DARK DIVINE

THE DIVINITIES
BOOK THREE

LIA DAVIS

Dark Divine

The Divinities, book 3

© copyright 2016 Lia Davis

Published by Davis Raynes Publishing Group, LLC

PO Box 224 | Middleburg, Fl. 32050

Cover by and Formatting by Glowing Moon Designs

www.AuthorLiaDavis.com

DARK DIVINE

HIS DARKEST SECRET IS REVEALED WHILE
HER GREATEST FEAR COMES TO LIFE.

New mother and Divinity, Lydia Rayners, is no stranger to heartache and loss. Her father, husband, and brother were taken from her by the demons, and now they want her son. Lydia will never let that happen, and she is determined to bring them down one by one—by herself if necessary. Her plans are going well until a certain sexy deputy discovers that she's the rumored demon slayer and is hell-bent on stopping her.

Witch and deputy sheriff, Zach Manus, has run from his past for too long and it's catching up to him now. He's determined to keep his dark family secret hidden as he fights for control over his emotions and growing powers. His darker side controlled him once before, and he won't let it happen again. But the closer he gets to Lydia, the more the darkness threatens to consume him, just as the gorgeous Divinity consumes his thoughts and threatens his resolve.

Zach is powerless to resist her, and while Lydia may understand him like no other, trusting her might unleash a new dark power that could destroy them both and put everyone they love in danger in the process.

CHAPTER ONE

*B*astards.

The two demons suspiciously lurking around the front of the hospital were up to no good. Lydia was sure of it. That was why she followed them—at a reasonable distance, of course—along the streets on the south bank of the St. Johns River.

Revenge coiled inside her, creating an angry ball of power waiting to be unleashed on the demons. They would not get away with destroying everything she loved. Or hurting any innocents in their paths.

Concern for the humans was the only thing holding her back. Her Divine power may be to heal, but pain from the loss of her family fueled the dark side of her power. The side she hid and had sworn to never use. Well, never use on an innocent. Demons were far from saints.

The hellspawns stopped suddenly. The one on the left, the taller one with shoulder-length blond hair, turned his head to peer behind them as if sensing something. *Her*. Lydia pressed her back into the cold brick wall and tried to slow her breathing and heart rate.

Warmth grew inside her and spread out to her palms. She kept her hands fisted by her sides, not wanting the demons to see the glow of the fire she'd called just in case the bastards decided to get stupid. She also didn't want them to see through the shadow spell she'd cast to conceal her presence from them.

After a few moments, one of the demons turned back around, shook his head, and both demons continued walking again. Lydia pulled the fire back a little and waited until the creep brothers rounded the next corner before following again.

There were too many humans around for Lydia to make her move. Even at midnight, downtown Jacksonville was hopping with humans enjoying the cooling fall night air and the array of festivities going on around the Riverwalk.

Pushing off the wall, she moved past a small

group of humans and stalked after the demons. As she'd suspected, they headed in the direction of the warehouse their not-so-mighty leader, Demetrius Grayson, used as a cover for his demonic operations.

A few blocks farther, and the hairs on the back of her neck rose as a dark, oil-like residue hung in the air. A low growl from behind her told her it was another demon.

Busted.

She whirled around and thrust her hand out, releasing the fire she'd called earlier. A softball-size fireball hit the demon in the chest. He managed to let out a scream before the flames spread over his body, and he *poofed* into a pile of ash on the ground.

She turned at the same time one of the other demons crashed into her, sending both of them flying into the brick wall. Pain ripped through her back and head. Reaching out, she placed a palm on the demon's chest over his heart and called her healer's gift. The gift she'd been born with and had been able to fully use by the time she was five. Even though her Divine gift was to magically heal, she could also reverse the healing process. In this case, she used it to stop the demon's heart from beating.

The demon's eyes widened when he realized what she was doing. He jerked and rolled out of her reach, but the damage was already done. She'd slowed his heart, and the blood flow through his body so much he couldn't move fast enough. Smiling, she flipped to her back and grabbed his ankle. It was enough contact for her to stop his heart altogether. He fell to the ground with a *thud*.

The silence of the night caught her off guard. She peered around at the empty alley. "Fuckin' chickenshit."

The third demon was nowhere to be seen.

And he'd seen her face.

Damn it!

She'd have to make sure she kept an eye out for that one. Because if her new extended family found out she'd been hunting demons on her own, they'd be livid, and most likely put a tail on her.

"Way to lose the trust of your fellow Divinities, Dia."

She sank farther back into the shadows so that any human walking by wouldn't see her dematerialize, and then focused on home.

A moment later, she stood outside the large barn in the backyard of her new home. Once the household of Kalissa and Khloe Bradenton, the large, three-story home was now the central base for the Divinities. They called it the Divinity House.

Up until earlier that year, they hadn't known there were other Divinities out there. Once Zach—the grandson of the priest and priestess of the Maxville Coven—set up an online community, they'd learned that there were others like Lydia, her mother, Ayden, and the Bradenton twins.

The other Divinities were well hidden in their covens and were happy to stay there. Too many of them were afraid of what this new uprising of demons would do to their safe havens.

Lydia didn't blame them. Especially after what had happened to the Oceanway Coven a few months ago. Demons had broken through the coven's wards, destroyed homes, and kidnapped two Dark Divine—the darker counterparts of the Divinities—children.

She shuddered at the memory. A moment later, Teddy-Bear, the Siamese twin hellhounds Hecate had appointed as the guardians of the Sinew—a marble-sized crystal sphere that held the world's magic—stuck their large heads out of the barn.

She ignored them at first, not wanting to hear a lecture at the moment. But it would come.

In true form, they stood about ten feet tall from paws to ears. They shared one body, but two independent heads with very different personalities.

They were both frightening and adorable in an over-sized dog kind of way.

Teddy shook his head as Bear said, "Dia, what have you been up to?"

She rolled her eyes. They knew what she'd been doing for months, but still pretended they didn't know. "Someone has to hunt the vile creatures down."

Teddy extended his head and sniffed. Lydia almost laughed. They'd smelled her from inside the barn with their supernatural senses. Teddy was trying to annoy her. "That is for the Divinities to do together, not for one of them to do alone."

"You're a mother, Dia," Bear said.

"Your son needs his mother alive," Teddy added.

Lydia fisted her hands and counted to ten. This argument was getting old. "My son is in danger as long as the demons walk the human realm."

Logan had been born with the dark rose, the symbol marking him as a Dark Divine. That meant her late husband, the man she'd trusted with her heart and soul had lied to her. He'd withheld his demonic nature from her.

Yes, she'd known he was a warlock—a dark witch who had been cast out by his or her coven. Many warlock children weren't given the choice to redeem themselves. Therefore, they carried the dark label simply because their parents were warlocks.

In Mikal's case, he wasn't only half demon, he was also the son of Khan, the ruler of the Underworld and the one responsible for the many coven attacks over the last few centuries.

She'd discovered that latter bit of information while going through Mikal's personal data files right after Logan was born.

"Logan is why I must do this. Khan will never take my son." The dark lord must never know Logan is his grandson.

She turned to the house, ending the conversation while noticing Ryn—a *Lackey* demon who'd helped her mom escape Demetrius's dungeon—lurking just inside the barn. Something bothered Lydia about the demon, but she couldn't quite put her finger on what.

Whatever. She quietly eased into the back door and crept up the stairs to her son's nursery. Peeking inside the room, she smiled at her baby boy peacefully sleeping in his crib.

Lydia walked over and bent to place a kiss on his head. "Mommy loves you, handsome."

Her chest filled with pride and overflowed with

love for him. She'd fight a thousand demons and die a hundred deaths to ensure that her son was safe.

And she'd do it with or without the other Divinities' help.

Zach paced his grandfather's man cave—the basement hidden under the stairs in the large foyer of the family home. He'd confined himself to the coven twenty-four hours ago because his grandfather, Noah, aka Papa, was out of the herb needed to perform the binding spell.

The spell that bound his dark side and kept it from coming out.

Fucking hell. Why now? He hadn't needed to go through the ritual in months. Not until Lydia had shown up. He ran a hand through his hair and pulled. His skin felt too tight, and his damn ears were pointed for gods' sake.

The door opened, making Zach turn toward it.

Papa came down the stairs, looked at him, and then shook his head. "The more you fight it, the stronger it becomes."

Zach snorted. "If I don't fight it, I may never be able to control it."

Noah went to the small altar against the center of the back wall of his study and sat a sachet of what Zach assumed was the herb on it.

"That is not true."

"I'm not taking any chances."

He'd lost control once. He'd been eight, and the darkness consumed him to the point where he'd killed his own father.

"Dark elves are not typically evil. The few that are, chose that path. The others live normal lives within covens that understand their abilities to weave demon magic." Noah turned to him, his brows drawn together, and stared at Zach as if he were trying to read him.

"I killed him."

His grandfather nodded and turned back to the altar. "Something that needed to be done," Papa spat out. "Your father chose his path and met his fate."

"The rage, the dark magic still haunts me." Zach dropped down onto the sofa and put his head in his hands.

He remembered everything from that night twenty-seven years ago as if it had happened yesterday.

He woke to his mother's cries of pain. She was pleading with someone to stop. "Please, Bobby, Zach is in the other room." Then the sound of a slap echoed through the house.

Anger stirred the dark magic within him. Zach gritted his teeth as he slipped from his bed and opened his bedroom door. From there, he could see into the dining room of the small cottage they lived in at the back edge of the Maxville Coven. When his father gripped his mother's throat, lifted her up, and then slammed her back into the wall hard enough to crack the drywall, something snapped inside Zach. Magic warmed him from the inside out, electrifying him. Consuming him.

He pushed the door open hard enough for it to slam into the wall. Then he marched out of his room into the dining room. "Dad, stop! You're hurting her!"

His father glanced at him from over his shoulder, his eyes pitch-black. "Go back to bed, Zachary."

Zach flicked his gaze to his mother. Tears streamed down her face, and she was fighting to breathe. She tried to speak, but no sound came out. His father was going to kill her.

Zach's vision grew dark, and he focused back on his

father as the rage built. Lifting his hands, Zach thrust them forward. Dark, grey energy flowed around his hands and shot out, hitting his father in the back, making him drop his hold on Zach's mother. She crumpled to the ground, taking in gasps of air.

The grey, smoke-like energy darkened and wrapped around his father's neck and chest. Zach lifted his hands higher, making the energy around them react to his motions. He threw his hands toward the wall, sending his father flying across the room and crashing into the drywall.

Unable to control the dark magic that consumed him, Zach moved toward the man he no longer considered his father. The only thought in his mind was that he needed to protect his mother from the monster.

Zach extended a hand toward his dad, closed his fist, and squeezed. Bobby's eyes grew round and changed back to the blue that matched Zach's. Still, Zach didn't let up until his father twitched for the last time and fell limply to the floor.

Zach shuddered and pushed away the memories. Lifting his head, he met his Papa's stare. "I don't want to be that out of control ever again."

Noah sighed. "I understand why, but I still don't think it's going to do you any good to perform the binding ritual. Besides, you were a child, and you remember it from a child's point of view. It appeared darker and scarier when you were eight."

Zach narrowed his eyes and studied his grandfather. At over three hundred years old, Noah was one of the first Divinities born. Or rather, blessed by the gods. Many witches believed that the Divinities were gifts from the gods and appointed as protectors, keeping humanity safe from the demons that walked in the human realm.

"What are you not telling me?"

Noah's lips twitched. "When an elf finds his mate, his magic becomes stronger, easier to manage."

Zach froze. No. He hadn't found a mate. Had he?

Only, his magic hadn't sparked to life since the night he'd killed his father. Until the day he met Lydia Rayners…

Fuck.

There was no way he was going to subject her to his dark side. The gods knew she'd been through Hades more times than anyone deserved.

She wasn't his magical mate.

She couldn't be.

CHAPTER TWO

"Here, kitty, kitty," Lydia taunted Khloe as she crouched down, bracing for impact.

Khloe let out a cackle and charged. Lydia jerked to the right a second before her friend made contact. Twirling around, Lydia was ready when Lo jumped toward her, tackling her to the ground. Lydia pressed her feet into Lo's stomach and flipped her over her head. Khloe landed on her back on the mat.

When Khloe jumped then flipped in the air to land on her feet, Lydia drew back out of reflex. Khloe's fangs had extended, and her eyes had changed to her inner jaguar's.

"No shifting, Lo," Lydia warned but didn't move out of her defensive stance. She'd use her Divine gift

13

to lay Khloe out if she had to. "Lo. Don't make me hurt you."

Shit.

Khloe moved forward, one hand shifting into a claw. Magic rippled over her skin.

Just then, Kristof Preston—Lydia's uncle, Divinity, and tiger shifter—stormed into the barn to stand between them, facing Khloe. "Stand down."

He spoke the words with a force that made Lydia want to bow down and submit to him.

Khloe stopped, studied him for a moment. Then she shifted back to her full human form and peered at Lydia. "I'm sorry…" Her bottom lip shook, and thunder rumbled overhead.

Lydia went to her and pulled her into a hug. "It's okay. You just got caught up in the moment."

Lydia walked Khloe out of the barn, ignoring Kris's growl as they went by.

"She needs to learn control," Kris called out, but Lydia ignored him. He might have taken over as Khloe's Alpha for her cat's sake, but he wasn't Lydia's Alpha.

She stopped and whirled around to face her uncle. "That's easy for you to say. You had your whole life to learn control. Lo's been a shifter for six freaking months. So back off."

When they reached the back porch of the main house, Jagger stepped out. He had Logan in his arms and a bottle in one hand.

Lydia smiled. "Look, Lo, your man looks good with a baby in his arms."

Khloe laughed. "Yeah? Well, he'll have to play with Logan and then my niece or nephew when Kalissa delivers."

Jagger lifted a brow. "We're not ready."

What he meant was that Khloe wasn't ready with all the changes she'd gone through over the past few months. Lydia didn't blame her really. She couldn't imagine what her friend had gone through finding out that her father was a jaguar shifter and having her own beast woken up at the same time.

Talk about a major life change.

Khloe trained with Kris three times a week on hunting, shifting, and learning to control the shift by regulating her emotions.

Logan whimpered, and Lydia took him from Jagger. "I'll take him. He may need changing."

She stepped around them and walked to the living room where she found her mom, Angelica, sitting in the recliner with a pair of headphones on. "Hi, Mom."

Her mother looked in her direction and smiled.

Lydia's heart ached. Her mother had been held captive by Demetrius, Khan's demon general. During Angelica's captivity, the demons had tortured her and blinded her with some kind of chemical.

Lydia had tried to heal her sight but failed. All she was able to do was make it so she could see shadows and shapes.

"Bring my grandson here," Angelica said, holding her arms out.

"Just a minute, Mom. I need to change him."

She walked over to the bookshelf to the right of the TV and picked up the wipes and a diaper, then sat sideways on the sofa and laid Logan on the cushion in front of her. "What are you listening to?"

Her mom pulled the ear buds from her ears and turned off the iPod. "An audiobook. They're great."

Lydia smiled. "I love to listen to them while jogging."

The sound of a truck coming up the driveway drew Lydia's attention. She finished diapering Logan and took him to his grandmother before going to the door.

She opened it, and a rush of excitement rolled through her. It was the movers she'd hired to bring the things she wanted from New York. There wasn't much she desired. Just the baby furniture and clothes and her bike, a black Ducati.

Oh, how she'd missed her motorcycle. She stepped out to greet the men. A few moments later, Khloe and Jagger came out just as Zach's black Camaro rolled to a stop next to the moving truck.

The passenger side door opened, and Bethany, Zach's older sister, stepped out. Lydia smiled, happy to see her new friend, and walked over to her.

Bethany returned the smile before sticking her head inside the car to get something out of the back seat. When she pulled back and straightened, she held a small dragon. He perched with his claws folded around her hand and wrist, and his long tail wrapped around her arm up to her shoulder. He couldn't be more than two feet tall.

And he was beautiful with his red scales that had a dark orange undertone. Turning his head, he met Lydia's gaze and blinked the brightest green eyes she'd ever seen.

"He's gorgeous." Lydia held out her hand tentatively.

Zach stopped next to her. "Careful. He's a fire breathing demon."

Lydia quickly pulled her hand back and turned to Zach as he started laughing. Bethany reached over and popped him in the back of the head. "Stop."

The dragon snapped his teeth at Zach and said, "No demon. You demon."

Shock made Lydia meet Bethany's gaze. "He speaks?"

Bethany scratched under the dragon's chin. "A little, but he understands everything we say. He mostly communicates through hand gestures and body language. But it does seem like he's picking up more and more words every day."

"Cool. Is he full-grown?"

"Yep. And he is house trained."

Lydia studied Beth for a few moments. "Why is he here?"

Beth smiled. "I'm hoping he'll be Angelica's familiar."

"Oh." At first, Lydia was confused. Had her mother asked for a familiar? It wasn't common for witches to take familiars nowadays unless they needed a boost while weaving magic, or if they'd lost one of their senses…

Lydia peered into Beth's smiling face. "He'll help her see again."

Beth nodded. "Yes, if they are compatible."

"Oh my gods, where did you get that

adorable dragon from?" Khloe asked as she flew out the front door and came to stand next to Lydia.

Bethany ran a hand over the dragon's head. "There is an elven couple in the coven that raises them on the other side. They heard about Angelica and gifted him to her."

"Aw. That was nice of them." Khloe reached out, and the dragon snapped its teeth. She jerked her hand back. "What the hell?"

Beth tapped the dragon on the nose lightly. "Behave."

"Demon."

Khloe laughed. "I'm not a demon."

Beth bit her lower lip before replying. "But your mate is."

Khloe's cheeks turned pink. "He's a good demon. A guardian for Hecate."

The dragon turned his head to the side then stretched out his neck toward Khloe and sniffed. "Jagger."

Spreading his wings wide, he hopped off Beth's arm and flew to the front door of the house. Jagger gave the small dragon a crooked grin. "Sal, what are you doing here?"

The dragon jumped and settled on Jagger's

shoulder as the Death Demon walked down the steps toward them.

"Ms. Rayners, where would you like this?"

Lydia pulled her attention away from the dragon and Jagger to turn to the movers, who seemed ready to haul ass. *Right. Human meets talking dragon.* She suppressed a laugh and offered them a sweet smile. Humans and their fears of the unknown. "You can unload the truck here. We'll take everything inside."

She could practically see the relief slide off them in sheets. Both men physically sagged into themselves as if they were glad they didn't have to enter the witches' house. She nibbled the inside of her lip to keep from saying anything.

Zach must have noticed because he moved closer to her, sending a wave of heat over her body. She took a deep breath to calm the rush of desire she always felt whenever he was near.

When the movers rolled the Ducati out, Zach whistled. "Holy shit. Is that yours?"

Lydia felt her cheeks rise as her smile widened. "Yep. I'm so glad I finally got her here."

There was nothing better than riding. The freedom she felt when she rode had helped her deal with the emptiness of losing her parents. Now that she was no longer pregnant, she could ride again.

Khloe walked over and nudged her arm. "Zach rides, too."

Zach shook his head. "I haven't had time lately with everything going on. Plus, my bike needs some work."

Khloe rolled her eyes. "He has an old BMW that he's restoring."

A tinge of jealousy stabbed at Lydia's belly. It bothered her slightly that Zach hadn't been the one to offer the personal information. Then again, she and Zach had only met six months ago. Why *would* he offer up the information?

Besides, it seemed as if he did everything in his power to avoid her. There were a few kind words here and there, and the occasional accidental brush of the hand or arm when he hung out at the house—which was often.

But that was it. It bothered her more than she realized.

Damn it. She hated this. The confusion, the need to be close to him, and the fear of his rejection.

A hand on her arm brought her out of her musings. She peered down and noticed it was Zach's hand on her forearm. Her Divine Rose on the under-side of that arm tingled and then warmed. She gasped and moved away from him.

"Lydia?" he asked and stepped forward.

She shook her head and dashed to the porch. Entering the living room, she forced a calm smile to her face and went to sit next to her mother. Logan's baby blue gaze found hers, and he giggled, holding out his chubby arms to her. Lydia's heart filled with joy and pride as she picked up her son and cradled him against her chest.

A moment later, Jagger, Khloe, and Zach came in, each carrying something the movers had dropped off. Frowning, she stood. "I can get those."

Zach shook his head. "Just sit. Beth is going to introduce the dragon to Angelica."

Lydia's mother gasped. "Dragon?"

Lydia patted her on the hand. "It's a pseudo-dragon, Mom. Bethany brought him to be your familiar."

Angelica smiled, obviously picking up on the fact that she would possibly be able to see again with the help of a familiar.

Beth walked around the sofa and sat on the coffee table in front of Angelica, Sal perched on her shoulder, his tail wrapped loosely around her neck. She reached out and took Angelica's hand in hers. "I want you to meet Sal. He's a pseudodragon."

Slowly, Beth moved Angelica's hand to Sal's

snout. The dragon leaned forward, sniffed her hand, then pressed his nose into her palm. "Sal, this is Angelica."

"Ange…Angel…" He shook his head and blew out a puff of smoke. "Say name."

Beth hid a smile and repeated Lydia's mom's name. "Angelica."

"No. Hard name."

Angelica laughed and cupped the dragon's long chin. "Sal. Call me Angie."

"Angie." He grinned, showing all his teeth, and snapped his jaw several times before unwinding his tail from around Beth and climbing down her arm toward Angelica. "I like."

He crawled into Angelica's lap and snuggled into her body.

Beth laughed and then clapped her hands. "This is great. I hadn't expected him to take to you so fast."

Angelica's eyes teared up, causing Lydia's to do the same. Logan patted her cheek as if sensing her mood. Smiling, she peered down at her baby and kissed his forehead. "Happy tears, Logan. Grandma will be able to see again."

Beth moved to sit on the sofa next to Lydia. "Angelica, the bond with a pseudodragon is different than that of a cat or other earth-born creature. The dragons choose their witches and initiate the bond. Sometimes, it's an instant bond, other times, it's a gradual bond. It all depends on how comfortable the dragon feels with you."

Sal rose up on his hind legs to be at eye level with Angelica, then placed his short front clawed feet on her face gently, and stared into her eyes. Lydia swore she saw the dragon's forehead scrunch into an angry frown.

A moment later, Sal tilted his head a little to the right, then his eyes started to glow. A hint of panic raced through Lydia but vanished when she peered into her mother's eyes. The milky appearance was gone, leaving behind the clear blue-green color that matched hers.

"Well, I think he's bonded with her. And, apparently, healed her injury. I didn't know he could do that," Beth said and leaned forward to peer at Angelica around Lydia. "How's your sight?"

Angelica smiled the brightest smile Lydia had seen since before her mother had been captured and stared at Sal. "You are a beautiful dragon."

The orange hue under the red in his scales darkened until his whole body was bright red. Lydia laughed. "I think he's blushing."

Beth nodded. "I believe so."

Angelica turned to Lydia, tears rolling down her face. Reaching out, Angelica touched her cheek. "My beautiful daughter." She looked down at Logan. "And my grandson."

Kris came in and placed his hand on her shoulders and bent down to kiss her temple. Angie faced him and cupped his cheek. "Kris."

Sal instantly wiggled himself between the couple, breaking whatever was about to happen between them. Lydia bunched her brows. She wasn't sure she wanted to know. Especially if it meant that Kris would soon be upgraded to her stepdad.

Zach, Khloe, and Jagger came back into the living room just as Kalissa and Melaina entered through the front door, carrying shopping bags. Kalissa nodded at everyone, stopping her gaze on the dragon still perched in Angelica's lap.

A smile formed on her lips, and she lifted her gaze to Zach. "Zach, Ayden said he'd be here shortly, but to start the meeting without him."

Lydia gathered Logan in her arms, stood, and picked up his burp cloth and a few toys scattered about. She started for the stairs when Zach spoke. "Lydia, I'd like for you to sit in on this meeting."

Her heart fell to her feet, and her stomach twisted in knots. Usually, it didn't matter if she sat in on the meetings or not, but she had an idea what this one was about. She so didn't want to be in the room.

Especially when there were two empaths present.

All it'd take would be one slip of emotion to give away the fact that she'd been out hunting demons.

CHAPTER THREE

*Z*ach watched Lydia turn toward him. She was nervous about something. He could sense it in the way her shoulders tensed when he'd asked her to stay. Come to think of it, she had been distant lately. Avoiding eye contact and skipping out on Divinities meetings.

Then again, so had he. With good reason.

What was *her* reason?

Bethany stood from her seat on the sofa and cast Zach a narrow-eyed glance before going to Lydia. "Let me take him for you."

Lydia offered Beth a warm smile and allowed her to take Logan. "Thanks. It's his nap time."

Beth cradled the baby, her motherly instincts kicking in. "No problem. I'll rock him to sleep."

Zach's sister disappeared up the stairs. Lydia came back into the living room and took a seat between Khloe and Angelica.

When Kalissa and Melaina made their way back from putting their bags up, Zach began briefing them on what he and Ayden had already talked about. "There is a rumor floating around Magical Enchantments that someone has been hunting and killing demons."

"And this is a problem, how?" Khloe asked.

Zach felt his lips twitch. He was so on board with Khloe's train of thought. He wanted to find out who was doing it and congratulate them. Hell, give them a hand running the bastards back to the Underworld. "It's a problem because humans are starting to notice strange things going on around downtown Jacksonville."

He ran a hand through his hair.

A spike of fear rolled off Lydia, making him meet her gaze. He stared into her green and blue eyes for several moments, trying to get a read on her emotions, but somehow, she blocked them from him.

Jagger spoke next, drawing Zach's attention from Lydia. "Lex heard the same rumor on the demon side. Only the demons have put a bounty on the so-called slayer."

Fuck. That wasn't good.

Lex was Jagger's brother, another Death Demon sent to help the Divinities in the war against the demons. Because he was also a *Porter*—a guardian of souls—he could freely walk between the three worlds. Lex used that ability to spy on the demons in the Underworld.

Khloe growled. Zach still wasn't used to her inner kitty cat. "Now that's a problem. I hope they don't think that gives their demonic asses a free ride to come to the natural realm. I just might have to go rogue myself."

Zach shook his head, ignoring Khloe for now. "We have to find out who this demon slayer is and put a stop to his or her demon hunting."

"Then we can recruit them and go after the demons as a team. That way, we can conceal it better from the humans." Khloe grinned when he stared at her, trying to give his best serious look. It was too hard with his best friend. She knew what buttons to push.

That meant she sensed too much of his dark-ening mood.

He knew it would only be a matter of time before

she figured him out. She was mated to a Death Demon, after all.

"Another problem we have is that there's been an increase in nighttime activity at Demetrius's warehouse. I don't like it." Zach took out his phone to check an incoming text.

It was his mother. *We need to talk when you get home.*

He sighed as he slipped the phone back into his pocket. He didn't want to talk with his mother, not about the elf thing, not now.

Lydia broke her silence. "Why don't we just blow up the damn building while everyone is inside? There goes a large percentage of our problem right there."

Khloe laughed and high-fived Lydia. "Now that's more like it."

Zach shook his head. When did he lose control of the meeting? "We can't just go in and blow up a building in downtown Jacksonville." Although, he kind of liked the idea.

Khloe shrugged, but her grin remained. "You can with the right plan and a spell large enough to block it from the humans."

Zach stilled and stared at the woman who used to be the first to fly out the door, ready to blow the demons to hell. Now, she sat there and talked about planning. He glanced over at her twin, who rubbed her pregnant belly and shrugged.

"I would have to agree with Lo on this one. I think we've stood by for too long. It's starting to bleed into the humans' lives. If they start learning about the demons walking their streets, we'll have bigger issues," Kalissa said.

And she was right. They had to act fast and keep the humans oblivious of the demons.

"And we have to make sure Demetrius is in the building when it blows," Melaina added.

Well, hell. Even the Divinity Elder was on board with this dangerous and risky plan. He took a deep breath and blew it out while he raked his fingers through his hair. "I guess we're going to do it. But I want this planned. Every 'i' dotted and 'T' crossed. No room left for mistakes. I don't want to lose another Divinity."

Everyone nodded their agreement so he ended the meeting. "We'll regroup once I talk to Ayden. Khloe, I want you to take a look at the warehouse's security, see if anything has changed. Kalissa, can you summon your ghost and see if she can tail Demetrius?"

Kalissa nodded. "Sure. Barbra loves to help."

Zach smiled. Barbra was Kalissa's ex-boyfriend's dead mother, who turned out to be half witch. She was now assigned as Kalissa and Khloe's spirit guide.

"Good. Lydia, can I speak to you for a minute?"

Lydia froze where she stood, darting her gaze to Khloe before meeting Zach's eyes. "Sure."

She hung back as the others left the room, the women with knowing smirks on their faces. Zach ignored it. It was not a big secret that there was an attraction between him and Lydia. Hell, they'd been skating around it for the last six months.

Zach was tired of skating, tired of running. Papa was right. There was no denying the pull Zach felt when he was near her.

That didn't mean they had to jump into anything right away. They could take it slow, have dinner, go for walks, and get to know each other. Then maybe she wouldn't flee when he told her he was half dark elf and that he'd killed his own father.

Once they were alone, he moved closer to Lydia and dropped the shield that blocked others' emotions. Allowing his empathic ability to pick up on her nervousness and worry.

"Why are you worried?"

She snapped her gaze to him, holding his stare

for several moments before speaking. "Logan. I fear the demons want him because he's a Dark Divine."

He knew that, but hearing her say it fueled his need to destroy the creatures and lock down the gates to the Underworld for good. He reached out and took her hand, linking his fingers with hers. Desire rolled off her in sweet waves. "Have dinner with me."

She shook her head. "Logan…"

He stepped closer to her, and she sucked in a breath. "Bring him."

She hesitated, and his heart sank as he feared she'd reject him. After a moment, she nodded. "Okay."

Relief washed over him, almost bringing him to his knees. "Good. We can leave when he wakes up from his nap."

She drew her brows together. "What about Beth?"

He smiled. "She's taking my car home, and we're teleporting. I just need to call my mom."

A shy smile formed on her lips. "I'll get Logan ready when he wakes up."

Fighting a moan, he watched as she rushed up the stairs. The sensation of her desire lingered in the air, flaring his hotter. He shook it off, pulled out his cell, and stepped out the back door.

He punched in his mom's number and waited, curious why she wanted to talk to him. That morning, she'd seemed fine, happy as usual. A sinking, dark feeling had settled in his gut since reading her text.

"Hi, baby."

Zach smiled and rolled his eyes. He'd accepted a long time ago that she would always consider him her baby even though he was the middle child. Bethany was her boo, and Annmarie was her princess. "Hi, Mom. Is everything okay?"

She paused briefly before answering. "When I logged into Magical Enchantment this morning, I noticed I had a private message. It was from Eleese."

The dark feeling turned to a gut-tightening fear as he opened his shields. His mom's voice trembled as she spoke, and Zach didn't like it. No one upset his mother. "What did it say, Mom?"

"It said for me to guard the children with my life. That the gates of hell will open." She released a sob and then asked, "What does that mean?"

He fisted his free hand at his side. He had a guess or two as to what it meant, but he needed to talk to Ayden first. Maybe he could see if Kalissa could use her Divine sight to see into the future. "I'm not sure yet. Have you shown the message to Papa?"

"Yeah, and he told me to tell you."

"Yeah. Thanks."

"Zach, what is it?"

He took a deep breath in then released it slowly. "Khan is cooking something. We don't know what, but I believe that message is meant to warn us. I think it's best to increase the wards around the coven. I have to go talk to Ayden. Love you, Mom."

"Love you, too. Do be careful."

"Always." He let out a slow chuckle in hopes of easing her anxiety. It was no use. She was a worrier. She was also a very strong, caring woman. Zach would do anything to keep her and his family safe.

The call ended, and he slid his phone back into his pocket just as Ayden stepped out on the porch. A quick glance, and Zach noticed his cousin was still in his uniform. "Mom got a message on ME." He repeated the warning his mother had relayed.

Ayden nodded while working his jaw. "The sooner we take care of Demetrius, the better. I'll have Khloe talk Lydia into taking Logan to the coven. Papa and Ma will protect him."

Zach nodded, knowing their grandparents would take Logan in without hesitation. He turned to walk back inside, but Ayden stopped him with a hand on his upper arm. "We're more like brothers than cousins, and not once have you told me about your elfin half."

Shocked, Zach narrowed his gaze on Ayden's. The glow of silver in the man's blue eyes told Zach that Ayden had used his Divine gift. After a moment, Zach sighed. "Did you tap into Kalissa's visions again?"

Ayden pursed his lips and hardened his stare. "You could lose your heart and humanity if you don't open up to your dark half. Embrace it, and use it to the Divinities' advantage, and then to your own."

Without waiting for a reply, Ayden released Zach's arm and walked back inside. Zach dropped his shoulders and stared out into the back yard. A moment later, Teddy-Bear exited the barn where they had their own place to sleep. They saw him and shook their heads. "Too many secrets."

Then they went back inside.

Zach ignored them. They wouldn't share what they knew anyway. Besides, he wasn't in the mood to bribe them. He already had to woo someone and win them over. Since Noah had mentioned that Lydia might be Zach's magical partner and possibly the one to soothe his inner demon, she was all he could think about.

The Divinity Roses on his arm weren't going away anytime soon.

He was blessed and cursed at the same time. He hoped she wouldn't run once she found out about his dark secret.

CHAPTER FOUR

*L*ydia stood in the middle of Zach's condo, amazed. "How long have you had this place?"

He slid the diaper bag from his shoulder and chuckled. The rough, masculine sound went straight to her core.

"I bought it several years ago after learning that Khloe had a unit in the building."

Lydia walked over to the wall of floor-to-ceiling windows to stare at the beautiful view of the St. John's River and downtown Jacksonville. The Maine Street Bridge was lit up with its blue lights reflecting in the water below it.

She felt Zach move up behind her. "It's beautiful at night."

She nodded. "So peaceful."

Zach moved to stand beside her, facing her. He ran a hand gently over Logan's head. She watched how he instantly looked relaxed. That was something she hadn't seen in him since the night they'd met.

He raised his lashes and held her stare. With a smile, he said, "Come on, you can lay him down in the spare room.

She followed him down a short hallway and then turned left into a…nursery. A *nursery*? Whirling around, she peered at him with a load of questions running through her mind. "This is more than a little creepy. Please tell me you're not hiding a wife somewhere and that you didn't lose a child—"

He pressed a finger to her lips, stopping her from saying anything more. "I've never been married, and have never gotten anyone pregnant."

"Then what is this?" She motioned to the room, keeping her voice calm and low so she wouldn't wake Logan.

He let his shoulders fall as he leaned against the doorframe. "I started on it after Cassia was born. Bethany had a hard time adjusting to motherhood at first and needed a quiet place to stay. So she stayed here with the baby."

She frowned. "Bethany? I can't imagine. She's a wonderful mother."

"She always has been. It's more like the witch's version of postpartum." Zach motioned Lydia inside.

He was not telling her something, but she let it go. For now. "But why haven't you taken down the crib? I mean, Cassia is sleeping in a toddler bed now, right?"

"I had a feeling that I'd need it." He rolled up the sleeve of the blue button-down he wore. When he got the sleeve rolled up to his elbow, he turned over his arm. Lydia gasped, her heart beating so fast that she feared it'd leap right out of her chest. On the inside of Zach's forearm were faded double roses connected to a vine that held a small bud.

She started to shake, but it wasn't out of shock. Fear, glee, and confusion consumed her. She'd tried to deny it over the last few months. Hiding her own new faded rose that had appeared next to the Divine Rose she'd been born with.

Zach stepped closer and spoke in her ear. "Yours appeared, too, didn't it?"

Afraid to speak, she just nodded. There was no use lying to him. He was an empath, he'd know before she spoke the words.

He gently took Logan from her arms and carried

him to the crib. When he came back to the doorway, she said, "I'm not moving in."

One side of his mouth lifted in a half-smile. "I didn't ask you to. I figured while we're getting to know each other, Logan could have a comfortable room to sleep in when we're here."

He started walking down the hall, and she followed. "What do you mean?"

"We can't ignore the pull to each other anymore. We are fated to be together." He turned suddenly, making her run into his chest. He gripped her elbows to steady her. "Say yes, Lydia. Be my girlfriend."

Girlfriend? She laughed. "That sounded so high school."

His grin widened into a smile. "I never said I was mature."

Trying to hold back another laugh, she flattened her palms on the cotton shirt covering his chest and pushed. He let her go and turned back toward the living room. She watched how his broad shoulders rolled as he walked. She allowed her gaze to roam over his back and down to his denim-covered ass.

Why was she debating it? She had nothing to lose by dating Zach. Well, nothing but her heart. Yet that had been broken so many times in the last few years, she wasn't sure it was still there.

"Zach, I'm not sure I have it in me to love anyone else."

He turned then and studied her, then reached out and ran his knuckle down her cheek. "I believe you are wrong. You're a wonderful mother, and I've seen the love you have for your own mother. I'm not asking you to fall in love with me just because the Fates think we are mates. I'm just asking for a few dates, phones calls, and I want to be able to touch you without feeling like I need permission."

That made her smile. She'd never seen this side of Zach. It'd always been the stressed out deputy, or the sarcastic witch that hung out at the house. She wanted to see more of this side of him.

She wanted to see all his sides.

Taking his hand from her cheek, she pressed a kiss to his palm and watched as he closed his eyes. "Yes, I'll be your girlfriend."

He flung his eyes back open, his brown irises a little darker than she'd seen them. She gasped as he wrapped his arms around her waist, tugged her into his body, and kissed her. When his tongue brushed along the seam of her lips, she opened and groaned as it darted inside.

Her nipples grew hard, and each movement of his chest against her bra sent hot pinpricks of desire over her skin. She cupped the back of his head and drew him in closer as she twined her tongue with his.

She felt him move her backwards. Her heart pounded as anticipation raced through her. For so long, she secretly wondered what it would be like to make love to Zach. Tonight, she wouldn't have to wonder anymore.

A little part of her warned that she was moving too fast, that it was too soon. She pushed all of that away, not caring. She needed this. Needed Zach.

Her back flattened against a wall, and Zach pressed his body to hers, placing his thigh between her legs. She broke the kiss with a soft cry as pleasure rushed through her. Peering into his eyes, Lydia saw swirls of gold in his brown depths, marking him as *magickin*—magic born.

His lips lifted in a sensual yet playful manner and sent scalding, liquid desire to her core.

Damn, she'd never been so hot for anyone.

"We shouldn't do this, not yet." He frowned.

She moved in and bit his bottom lip and tugged. He groaned and ground his hard, denim-covered erection into her stomach. After she'd released his lip, she said, "You don't get to back out now."

The gold in his eyes intensified, almost dominated the brown. He raised a brow, then nipped at her nose. "I was just giving you a chance to back out."

She felt the corner of her lips lift. "I don't back down from anything. Especially from something I want."

Suddenly, the room faded out, and she felt as if she were being pulled through thick jelly. In a flash of soft, white light, the bedroom next to the nursery came into view. She smirked and held Zach's gaze. He'd teleported them into his bedroom.

He walked her backwards until the backs of her thighs touched the bed. He pushed her, and she fell backwards on the mattress. Lydia's breathing came in long, deep gasps as she watched him kneel down in front of her and start to remove her jeans.

His fingers grazed her belly, and a spark of magic tingled her skin. It didn't hurt. It was more like static electricity. But it concerned her. Zach was holding on to too much magic.

She grabbed his hand, drawing his attention to her. "If you need to release some magic, I can help."

Being a magical healer meant she could help

other *magickin*, witches in particular, in a number of power transfers. She wasn't too sure how it worked exactly. She could absorb the overflow of magic and convert it to her natural ability to heal.

He fell silent and averted his gaze. Fearful she'd ruined the mood, she sat up and cupped his face. "I'm a Divine healer. I can take any power overflow you need to release. No questions. No judgment."

He studied her for a moment and then nodded. She gave him a quick kiss on the lips and lay back on her elbows.

Zach resumed the slow movements of undressing her. This time, starting with her tennis shoes. She held in her amusement and just watched. He held her gaze as he let her shoes hit the floor, then moved up her legs to undo her jeans. She laid back and lifted her hips so he could pull them off, along with her panties.

She felt his teeth nip at her inner thigh and she jumped, a hot shudder rolling through her. He trailed light kisses up her leg to her sex. His warm tongue licked her clit, and she bit her bottom lip to keep from crying out and waking the baby.

She tingled everywhere, and she could feel Zach's power reaching out to hers. The power was warm and soothing as it wrapped around her body until it covered every inch of her. She opened up to his magic, to him, allowing her own gift to give him the release she could feel he needed.

A need that was raw, sensual, and a little dark.

She didn't focus on the dark. Instead, wrote it off as the stress they had all been under the past months.

The power transfer was a natural part of sex among magical lovers, especially soul mates like she and Zach. By allowing this transfer, she was accepting what the Fates had in store for them. They were magical mates, life partners.

Another wave of pleasure washed over her as Zach sucked and licked her to orgasm. She gripped a handful of his hair and rocked against him, riding the current until she couldn't stand it anymore.

Zach gave one last lick, making her shudder before he stood and removed his clothes.

He settled over her but didn't touch her. She reached out to cup his face, but he grabbed her wrist and held it against the mattress over her head. A shot of excitement burned within her, calling her element of fire closer to the surface.

Fear flashed, and she started to yank on her hand. She had to get a handle on the fire before it took over. It'd happened before with Mikal, and she'd ended up burning his chest with her hand.

Zach pressed the lower half of his body to hers. "Stop fighting it, Dia."

She shook her head. "I don't understand why the fire is rising. I didn't call it."

"I know. Just let it go. I have the ability to shield, remember?"

Yeah, she remembered, but that only gave her a little comfort.

She nodded and relaxed under him. He lowered his head and pressed a kiss above her left breast, then her right, before moving down to take a nipple into his mouth and suck. Her body jerked under his hold, and her pussy ached for him to be inside her.

Moving her hips against him, she groaned. "Please."

"Patience," he purred into her ear right before he gently bit down on her earlobe. Her skin felt tight and much too warm.

"I don't want to be patient. I need you. Now."

He let out a low, husky laugh and kissed her neck just as he lifted his hips and thrust into her. She let out a muffled scream of pleasure as he filled her and stretched her in the best possible way.

Her fire licked at her just below the surface but

didn't threaten to consume her. Still, her body temperature was much higher than Zach's. She couldn't help but wonder if he minded.

Zach bit down on her shoulder, bringing her back from the fear of losing it. "I'm fine. I can feel your worry. All I want to feel is your pleasure. Now."

Gods, his demands turned her on. Who knew that the sarcastic deputy could be so controlling in the bedroom. She lifted and bit his ear. "What if I don't?"

He thrust deeper inside her, making her cry out. "That's better," he teased and claimed her mouth.

He dipped his tongue inside, and she twirled hers around his in an erotic dance. His tempo increased, pushing her further over the edge. She met each thrust and scored his back with her nails as another orgasm crashed into her.

Zach followed with one of his own, and she wrapped her arms around him, hugging him close as he shuddered and rode out the last waves of his orgasm.

He settled on his side next to her and drew her close so they spooned with his leg tucked between hers. "That was…"

Lydia took a breath. "Yeah."

CHAPTER FIVE

*S*amoan Greyson paced her father's laboratory in the basement of his downtown warehouse, trying not to kill the Divinity sitting at one of the workbenches.

Desiree Sanders wasn't only a Divinity, she was also a *Porter*. Commonly known as a soul keeper. She could pass through to each of the three worlds at will, yet she couldn't recharge the piece of crystal that had once been a part of the Sinew—the crystal sphere that held all the worlds' magic. Samoan was about to call her on her bullshit.

Frustration wore on her last nerve. Storming out of the room, Samoan headed down the hall to her father's office. She had a mating ceremony to plan. Wasting time watching Desiree pretend to be unable to recharge the crystal was hazardous to Samoan's mood—and the witch's life.

You can't kill the witch. Not yet. Father has a plan. Samoan rolled her eyes. Dear ol' dad always had a plan, and backup plans for his failures. However, he did seem to get the job done, at least most of the time. When he wasn't treating her like a spoiled child and barking orders at her every time she was near anyway.

That would all change once she'd mated Khan and ruled the three worlds by his side. Then, Daddy would take orders from her.

Thoughts of being queen of the Underworld lifted her mood. She smiled as she entered her father's office and dropped into a chair across from him at his mahogany desk.

Demetrius lifted a brow. "Do you have news?"

She shrugged. "No. I'm just thinking about my future mate."

"Good. I'm glad you accept him."

If only he knew. "He's perfect for me, and everything I want in a mate. I'm grateful he accepted me."

Demetrius nodded, and a small smile lifted his lips. "Khan approached me."

Yes, she knew that but didn't dare let her father know they had planned this union since Liam's fuck-up a few months ago. And Demetrius's failure to control the situation. Samoan had approached Khan with a deal too good for him to pass up. A queen that was more ruthless than he. It was a bonus that she and Khan were fated mates.

Another secret she'd keep from her father. For now.

"Oh, there is one small thing. The witch sent her warning message under her mother's account in the witch social network." Another giddy feeling fluttered in her belly.

"Good. Now, the Divinities will be scrambling, preparing for an apocalypse."

"Leaving them vulnerable to attack." And Samoan could take Logan and deliver him to his grandfather. A gift to her future mate. But first, she'd have to take care of Lydia. "There is the issue of the rogue huntress."

"Curse her. If it's blood she wants, make her crave it."

A wicked grin tugged at her lips. "You are a genius." She leaned forward to see what had him so preoccupied. Usually, he would be ordering her to keep the *Lackeys* in line or organizing a *Regal* attack or something. "What are you working on?"

He glanced at her and then sat back in his leather

office chair. "Did you know that Siamese hellhounds can separate from each other for short periods of time? They will do so to confuse their opponents during battle."

"I have seen the Divinities' hounds do it."

"Have you seen the Sinew on them?"

She stared for several long moments before she caught on to where he was going with this. "No, I haven't, but I bet it's there. They are the bound guardians."

Meaning they couldn't let it out of their sight. Ever. Or weren't supposed to.

"Exactly. I'm going to capture the hounds and take the Sinew."

Lifting a brow, she asked, "How are you going to do that? We've already tried to breach the Divinity House, but there is always someone there, and they keep strengthening the wards."

Demetrius let out a chuckle. "After your little message, they will be plotting to come to us."

"We'll need to figure out when and where." Samoan thought about it for a moment. The *Lackey*, Ryn, came to mind. It was almost too easy.

She stood, and her father asked, "Where are you going?"

With a smirk, she replied, "To find our friend, Ryn, and torture some info from him."

"You are ruthless." He sat back in his leather chair with a wide grin. "I'm glad you are on my side."

He was wrong. She was on no one's side. He'd taught her that. *Trust and depend on no one. Only then will you be free and not be disappointed when those closest to you betray you.* That had been his advice during training since she was old enough to walk.

She had lived by those words. Especially after watching her father become weakened by her mother's death. Samoan vowed to never love that deeply. That's why mating Khan was perfect for her. They could appreciate each other's love for world domination and destruction.

A match made in hell.

Desiree tapped her fingers against the desk she

pretended to work at, trying to think of a way to fool Samoan into thinking she was making progress on the stone. Gods, she hated this. The betrayal to her fellow Divinities and *magickin* ate at her. But what choice did she have? Khan had her son, holding him as collateral in exchange for her charging the piece of Sinew and giving him intel on the Divinities.

Please, goddess, help me. Direct me in the right direction.

She picked up her phone and called her mom. Eleese picked up on the second ring. "Hi, hon."

"Hi, Mom. I'll be heading home soon, and wondered if you needed anything."

"No, I'm good."

The tremble in her words put Desiree on edge. "Is everything okay?"

There was a slight hesitation before her mother answered. "I'm not sure. I think I'm being paranoid since the break-in."

Desiree's heart broke, and guilt threatened to steal her ability to breathe. "We're safer now than before. Plus, the Divinities are close to ending the war."

"Gods, I hope you're right." Eleese released a soft sigh. "I'll talk to you when you get here."

"Okay, Mom. Love you."

As soon as she'd ended the call and laid her phone back on the table, power zapped through the room, and the door flung open, slamming into the wall. Whirling around, Desiree glared at the she-demon filling the doorway.

Samoan moved faster than Desiree could track, gripping her by the throat and lifting her off the chair. "You are withholding information from me."

Desiree laughed, humorless and a little evil. "Of course, bitch. Did you really think I would tell you everything?"

Samoan's eyes flashed crimson, and one side of her mouth lifted. "No, I guess not." She tossed Desiree back. She hit the wall and crumpled to the ground. "I have a secret, too. Your son is really dead."

Pain and rage swirled inside Desiree. She'd suspected Samoan had lied all along but hope that she'd once again hold her son had blinded her. With her telekinesis, she picked up the crystal and suspended it in mid-air between them. Focusing, she put everything she had into it. The stone glowed red, power filling it. Samoan reached out for it but jerked back a moment before the small piece of the Sinew shattered into dust.

Desiree smirked as she rose to her feet. Swiping her hand through the air, she blasted Samoan with an energy ball. The demoness flew into the wall across from Desiree. Walking to the door, Desiree glared at her. "I have secrets, too, bitch."

A moment later, she materialized in her house at the Oceanway Coven. She collapsed into a ball in the middle of her living room floor. Her heart breaking all over again. Mathew had been two years old when he fell ill. Nothing she did made him better. Then she'd met Samoan about six months later, not knowing she was a demon.

Matty went into a coma, and Samoan had said she'd take him to a safe place to heal. Desperate to save her son, Desiree had let the demon take him. However, she'd lied to her family and coven, and told them Matty had passed on. Samoan had fooled Desiree into believing she was doing the right thing.

Gods, she'd been so stupid, and so desperate to have her son cured and back at home.

I'm such a fool. She should have been able to see through Samoan's glamour. But she hadn't, not before it was too late and she was trapped into working for the demons.

Matty would have turned ten in a few months.

Taking short, hiccup-like breaths, she sat up and conjured the phone she'd left in the lab. After staring at the numbers for several long moments, she dialed the only person she might be able to trust.

"Hello." The rough, deep, male voice sent a shiver down her spine. When she didn't say anything at first, he growled. "Speak, female."

"Lex, I need your help."

She hung up, knowing all too well the Death Demon would materialize in her living room in a moment or two.

Fear froze her in place. She just hoped Lex would help her and not kill her for the betrayal and lies she'd built her life on.

CHAPTER SIX

*E*very muscle in his six-foot-seven-inch body tensed up at the broken sound of Desiree's voice. She was in pain, and all Lex wanted to do was hunt down the SOB who'd hurt her. For her to reach out to him of all people told him that she was in some deep shit.

When he materialized in her living room, his heart dropped to his feet. Fury mingled with concern, battling for dominance. Since he'd lost his own family, he'd sworn to never become attached to anyone ever again. The pain from the loss had damn near driven him insane.

Jagger and Hecate were the ones to reach into the dark place he'd retreated to and drag his ass back to reality. Still, Lex kept his emotions on a short leash.

Squatting next to Desiree's curled up body on the floor, Lex brushed the hair out of her face. Her eyes were filled with tears. Her cheeks wet. Sadness choked him. Why was it so hard to keep the damned emotions locked up around her?

Without speaking, he sat with his back against the sofa and legs straight out while lifting her into his lap. Her strawberry scent coiled around him, stirring up desire along with the urge to kill every demon on earth and in the Underworld.

After what seemed like hours, Desiree spoke. "I have a son. He turns ten on the Solstice." He nodded but sensed she wasn't done, so he remained silent. "He was taken from me when he was two. An illness took him."

She shook her head and continued. "No, the illness didn't take him. Samoan did. She tricked me, told me she could cure him."

The more she talked, the more the fury mounted inside him. Samoan, Demetrius, and Khan were going to die. Desiree told him about the lies she'd told her coven. And how she'd worked under Samoan's command.

When she stopped talking, he pursed his lips and worked his jaw. She'd betrayed her own kind.

Worked with the demons, feeding them information and helping them gain power.

He should be furious with her. Hell, it was his duty to kill traitors like her. And she knew it.

"Why haven't you sought help before now?"

She gave a half shrug. "I was in too deep."

"And now?"

"Now, Samoan knows I'm a *Porter*, and I have the power to recharge any part of the Sinew." She raised her head and stared into his eyes. "I shattered the crystal."

"She'll be looking for you. Might just kill you."

She averted her gaze. "I know. But I can't shake the feeling that Matty might still be alive. That he survived the illness. Despite what Samoan told me."

"Your son was never sick."

"What?" She jerked her gaze to his and frowned.

"Who was his father?"

A spike of embarrassment colored her cheeks. She pushed out of his arms and stood. "I don't know."

He raised a brow as he stood in front of her. "Do you have a guess?"

"I was nineteen. Too young to know what I wanted. I was trying to fit in with everyone at college." The next part was muttered, but Lex heard it loud and clear. "There was a party and a little too much fun with a couple of warlocks."

If jealousy hadn't raised its head, Lex would have laughed. Besides, sex was a natural thing. To find another *magickin* to share the pleasure with was a bonus. Gods knew he'd had his fair share of no-strings-attached lovers. "And you've never seen them again."

"I didn't intend to." She blew out a breath. "I was craving the power exchange. I was just too high to realize they had other plans."

A knowing settled over him. They'd gotten her pregnant on purpose. But for what reason? "Have either of them tried to contact you?"

"No, which is weird if they meant to get me pregnant."

She wrung her hands and began to pace. He could tell she was churning the scenario over in her mind. He stepped closer to her and reached out to grab her hands. Upon contact, she stilled and met his stare. "*Porters* don't get sick, ever. If they are mixed with a demon or something darker, they can go through a transformation."

Her eyes grew large, and her bottom lip trembled. "Then he *is* alive. I have to go get him."

Lex gripped her arms, keeping her in place. "You will not go alone."

"Then let's go."

He shook his head. "The Divinities need to know about this. All of it. Besides, if I'm right about him going through a transformation, then he wouldn't know who you are. He won't be your son anymore."

She narrowed her blue eyes at him. "He will always be my son."

"Wait for the right time. Get yourself caught, and I'll come for you. The demons can't know you are coming." He hoped she'd caught on to what he was trying to say. There were too many ears and eyes everywhere. The presence of demons around the coven made his skin crawl. "Tell your mother to strengthen the wards. Then wait for my call."

She frowned but nodded. "I hope your plan is better than it sounds. Believe it or not, I don't have a death wish."

His lips twisted. "There will be no dying on my watch."

CHAPTER SEVEN

*L*ydia woke with a start. At first, she didn't know where she was, then she remembered the wonderful evening she'd spent with Zach. With a smile, she snuggled into the covers. Peace settled over her, and she took in the quiet of the apartment.

Wait. It was too quiet. *Logan!*

She flung off the covers and raced to the nursery. Logan wasn't there. Fear froze her blood as she turned and ran down the hall. When she reached the living room, she stilled, frozen in awe. Zach held Logan in his arms, feeding him a bottle, and humming softly as he rocked back and forth in front of the wall of windows.

Her heart bloomed with love while other parts of

her longed for a repeat of the night before. Shaking off the naughty thoughts, she stepped farther into the room. Zach turned and met her gaze. His brown depths had swirls of gold that reflected the natural morning light.

Logan let out a soft whine, drawing her attention to him. She advanced to them and took Logan from Zach's arms, careful not to touch the male. Her skin was still too sensitive from the power exchanges during the many times they'd made love.

Abruptly, she twisted around to make her escape. "He needs to be changed."

"I'll fix breakfast. Do you have a preference?" Zach stalked to the kitchen.

Lydia tried not to notice the flicker of hurt that had crossed his features and the disbelief in his tone before he turned away. Her own feelings worked overtime. She was angry at the demons, sad for her loss, and the damn new mom hormones made her want things she shouldn't.

Her vision blurred as she changed Logan's diaper. It was all the sexy witch in the kitchen's fault. Why did he have to be too good to be true?

What was she thinking? She couldn't have feelings for Zach. Not yet. Logan's future had to be secured first before she could think about her own happiness. A tear rolled down her cheek as Zach's earthy scent filled the room.

The man made it hard to focus on her mission. Wiping her cheek, she lifted Logan in her arms, cradling the bundle of sweet baby to her chest. Oh, how she wished Mikal could have seen his son. More tears filled her eyes.

Zach stepped to her, his brows drawn. "What is it?"

Lydia shook her head, not wanting to talk about it. Even though she and Mikal weren't magical mates, she'd still cared deeply for him. Zach stroked her cheek with his knuckles. "I wish I could take your pain away."

She stepped around him. Being close to him overwhelmed her. His scent lured her in, as did his smile and the longing that mirrored her own in his brown gaze. "I can't do this."

"Do what?" He closed in on her.

"Us. Not now." She stepped out of his reach. "It's too much, too fast. I'm not ready."

With a single thought, she teleported herself and Logan to her bedroom at the Divinity House. She needed to get away from Zach to think, to refocus.

After kissing Logan on the forehead, she laid him

in his crib and then traced his small round face with her index finger. *My sweet angel.*

Suddenly, the natural light from the window darkened. She leaned over the crib to move the sheer curtains to the side to gaze out. Dark, unnatural clouds covered the sky, blocking the sunlight. Lightning flashed outside the window, followed by the *boom* of thunder. She jumped back out of reflex, and a chill skittered up Lydia's spine.

This isn't good.

"That wasn't me!" Khloe called from downstairs.

Lydia's lips twisted in amusement. The playfulness was short-lived, as a moment later, her bedroom door slammed shut, and the power cut off, bathing the room in darkness.

Forming a small fireball to illuminate the space, she checked on Logan before going to the door. She grabbed the handle and jerked. It didn't budge. Panic burned in her gut. She wasn't claustrophobic or anything, but the idea of being trapped didn't settle well with her. Especially since the dark energy she'd felt a moment before the lights had gone out was growing.

A moment later, a ghostly figure took form in front of her. She willed the candle on her dresser to light and readied herself to throw the ball of fire at the newcomer. The ghost wasn't friendly. She wasn't sure he was even a ghost. *Shadow demon.* She bared her teeth and formed a second fireball.

The demon laughed, an evil screech-like sound that made her skin crawl. *Worse than nails on a chalkboard...* The transparent creature spoke without moving his lips. "Fire will not harm me, witch."

She feared that was the case. Yet, she schooled her features, to keep the demon from knowing she was scared shitless for her son's life. Instead, she sent her best friend a thought. *Khloe, I have a shadow demon with* Regal *powers in my room.*

Yeah, we're dealing with our own shit. Be with you soon. Khloe's last statement was said with snark, as if she were enjoying herself far too much.

Studying the demon, Lydia narrowed her eyes and noted that he wasn't in any hurry to attack. Or, at least, that was what he wanted her to think. "You're not leaving this house alive."

"We'll see." The arrogant bastard smiled.

Think, Lydia. She stepped back then slid to the side so she could see Logan out of the corner of her eye. A slow, white glow came from his bed. Sparing a quick glance, she gasped and immediately threw up a circle around herself and the demon.

Confusion regarding why and how Logan could

possess power at only six months old fueled her fear. The only thought she had was to keep the demon from her son. "What do you want?"

The demon reached out and grabbed her by the throat, then lifted her off the ground. She clawed at his wrist and fought to take deep breaths.

She would not die!

Gazing into his black eyes, she wrapped the fingers of both hands around his forearm. Gathering all her anger and pain, she formed a large, dark ball of power. "You will not leave here alive." She repeated her earlier words as she forced the power out of her hands and into the demon.

Instead of slowing the demon down, or weakening him as she'd hoped, the energy ball seemed to fuel his strength. What the hell?

He let out the screech-like, wicked laugh again and raised his free hand to poke at her circle. The sheer walls fell like a bubble bursting. *No. No*!

She was powerless against him. A weak healer. Fear burned her insides.

Logan cooed, and the demon turned his head toward the baby. Lydia kicked her legs and clawed at him, hoping to draw his attention away from her son.

With a flick of his wrist, the demon thrust Lydia

into the wall opposite Logan. Pain shot up her back and sliced through her skull. Taking deep breaths, she pushed away the agony and stood.

The demon was standing over Logan's crib with his head cocked to the side. Lydia screamed, "Don't touch him!"

When she moved to rush forward, the demon waved a hand in her direction. She froze in place. *Gods, no*! Her stomach soured as she watched the demon reach into the crib and pick up Logan.

She screamed, hoping someone would hear the panic in her voice. That was if the others weren't dead...and she was all alone. Helpless to save her son. Just as she was to help her husband and her brother.

What was wrong with her? *I am stronger than this.*

She focused on the demon holding her son. The bastard had put those doubts in her mind. He was trying to break her down. "Logan, Mommy is here."

At the sound of her voice, Logan laughed. The first one she'd heard from him. Tears formed and spilled over her lashes. But she also noticed how the demon snarled at the laugh. That gave her a thought. If the creature grew stronger at her rage, then her son's pure love would be the demon's downfall.

"Logan, Mommy loves you." Logan smiled and

glanced at her. She smiled back and added in a sweet, cooing sound, "Give the ugly demon a hug. He needs love."

The baby looked at the demon and reached out with his hands. When the baby's chubby fingers touched the demon's face, Logan smiled wide. The demon, however, screamed and jerked Logan away from him, holding the baby at arms' length.

"Don't hurt my baby!" Anger boiled in her blood.

The demon screamed again as Logan touched his arms. The power holding her in place slipped as if the demon's focus were on something else. Then Lydia saw it. The glow from Logan's hands. Her son was using the demon's power against him.

Adaptability. But how? Logan was too young, wasn't he?

A moment later, the bedroom door flew open, and Zach rushed by her before she'd realized what was happening. Khloe was at her side in a heartbeat. "Are you okay?"

A flash went off, drawing Lydia's attention to where the demon had stood a moment before. Zach's back was turned to her, but Logan gazed at her from over Zach's shoulder. Her heart ached while her body sagged in relief that her son was safe.

As she approached, she sensed something was wrong with Zach. Had he been hurt? "Zach?"

He shook his head. Khloe cleared her throat behind them. "It's time to stop hiding, Zachary."

A chuckle escaped him, but it wasn't his normal carefree laugh. He turned, not meeting Lydia's gaze. A part of her was hurt, the other part shocked at what she saw. Zach had pointed ears, and his skin seemed to shimmer like an elf's. The fact that he hadn't shared this part of him with her hurt deeper than she wanted to admit.

"Who's hiding? I'm right here." A failed attempt to be sarcastic on his part. His tone held too much of an edge.

Lydia glanced at the spot where the demon had stood earlier. A heavy magical residue floated in the air; otherwise, there was no sign of him. Now she wondered what Zach had done to save Logan. Closing the gap between them, she took Logan from Zach and then left the room without a word.

Emotions ran wild inside her. She wanted to yell at Zach for hiding who he truly was from her. Yet, that wouldn't be fair considering she had a secret, too. One she wasn't ready to reveal. One she wouldn't share until her family was avenged.

A few moments later, she entered the living room

and frowned. Melaina, Barbra, and Lydia's mom were straightening the overturned furniture. Sal flew around the room, muttering "demons" over and over.

Angelica glanced up, sighed in relief, and advanced to Lydia. Her mom pulled her and Logan into a hug. "I'm so glad you are safe."

"I'm glad no one was hurt."

Her mom pulled back, her brows drawn together. "The demons down here were a distraction. To keep us busy while you were trapped with the shadow demon."

Lydia nodded. It was what she had thought, too. "The demon never expected Logan to have the power of adaptability."

"So young?"

Kalissa stepped out of the master suite connected to the living room. She met Lydia's gaze and spoke telepathically to Lydia. *"Zach's not the only one with secrets."* Lydia broke the eye contact while Kalissa said out loud, "Ayden told me he'd always been able to use his gift of adaptability. Noah said it isn't uncommon for some Divinities to be born with their gifts."

"And since Logan is a Dark Divine, he will develop his powers sooner," Mel added.

Lydia nodded and sat on the sofa, hugging her son tightly to her chest. The feeling of helplessness still clung to her. She didn't have a useful gift. At least, it wasn't helpful when fighting demons unless she could get close enough to touch them. The demons knew it.

Apparently, they'd stop at nothing to get at her son.

"I want Logan's powers bound."

Khloe growled as she entered the room. "Don't think about hiding who he is from him."

Lydia met her friend's teal stare. "Not from him, from the demons. Bind his powers and hide his magical signature." She looked at Mel and asked, "That can be done, right?"

With a short nod, Mel used telekinesis to move the armchair back into its place. "Yes. It may take the power of three. Noah, Vanessa, and I could do it. I believe we could also make it temporary. Noah will know what to do."

Lydia glanced at the staircase and wondered if Zach had teleported home since he hadn't come downstairs with Khloe. Pushing away the ache in her heart, she focused back on the group. "Could he stay at Maxville Coven?"

Mel smiled. "I'm sure Noah and Vanessa won't have it any other way."

A sense of sadness settled over Lydia. It wasn't a secret that the priest and priestess of the Maxville Coven were trying to conceive with no luck. It was putting a lot of stress on the couple. Lydia had offered to help, and had even examined Vanessa. But Lydia couldn't find any reason why she couldn't get pregnant. It was strange.

As if picking up on her train of thought, Khloe chimed in with, "Besides, Papa and Ma would love the chance to have a baby in the house."

Mel stood. "I'll call Vanessa and get everything arranged for the ritual. Is midnight tonight too soon?"

Not soon enough. "No. That would be perfect."

CHAPTER EIGHT

*Z*ach entered the Daniels' house in the Maxville Coven just as his younger sister, Annmarie, walked into the foyer. She lifted her head from her tablet to gaze at him and stopped. A smirk formed, and she said, "I guess the cat is out of the bag. No, wait. That would be elf."

She burst out in laughter, which made Zach smile. Trying to hide his amusement, he advanced to her and snatched her tablet from her. "You think you're funny, huh?"

"Oh, I'm much funnier than you." She gripped her tablet, but he didn't release it. Instead, he hugged her close. "What is it, Z?"

Her concern and love helped to ground him. When he'd walked through the door, his intent had been to head straight to the gym. Toasting the shadow demon in Lydia's room hadn't eased his need to protect. And when Lydia had walked out without a word… He didn't know what to do with all the emotions that were built up inside him.

Plus, not knowing what she thought about his secret ate at him. He'd felt her hurt but couldn't decipher if it was directed at him or herself.

Taking a deep breath, he released his sister. "Lydia almost lost her son tonight. I was almost too late getting to them."

Annmarie poked him in the chest. "Don't you dare take the blame. You did get there, didn't you? And I take it you outed yourself in the process."

He just stared at her. She rolled her eyes and continued. "I may only be here on the weekends, but I know what's up. Besides, Mom and Beth keep me in the loop." She smiled widely before rising on her toes to kiss his cheek. "Everything happens for a reason. You just have to wade through the shit before finding out what that reason is."

"When did you grow up?"

She pushed at him playfully. "Way before you did."

He reached for her, and she darted out of his way. Just then, he felt his mother's presence. Glancing up, he met her stare from the family room entrance. Her blonde hair fell over her shoulders in waves. The loving smile she gave him reached her blue eyes.

Zach loved seeing his mom happy. Thinking back to the day his father had died, Zach knew if he had a chance to go back in time, he wouldn't change a thing. Well, except to tell his younger self that it wasn't worth hiding who he was.

Annmarie glanced to their mom and then back to Zach. "She's been waiting for you to get home."

He nodded, and Ann left the room. Even though their mom wasn't a Divinity, she was very intuitive. Plus, Lynzee Manus was his mother. They shared a magical bond like all *magickin* did with their children.

When she turned to go into the family room, he followed. "I don't like the ears."

"They are a part of you. However, you can use glamour to hide them in public." Lynzee sat in an armchair she used for reading or knitting. She grabbed her knitting needles and picked up where she'd left off on the baby blanket she was making for Logan.

After a few moments of silence, Zach stretched out on the sofa. "Lydia didn't say anything. She stared at me, took Logan, and left the room."

"She'll need time."

"She deserves someone better."

His mom raised her brows at him. "You would really watch her settle down with someone else?"

Blowing out a breath, he covered his face with his arm. "No. I just…don't want to hurt her."

"You won't. Unless you push her away."

"What if I turn out to be like *him*?"

She laid the blanket and needles down and stared at him. "Your father was insane long before I met him. We weren't magical partners. I was very young, and was blinded by his good looks and charm. A childish crush for the older man with pretty words."

Anger rolled off her, mixing with a sorrow she hid from everyone until the subject of his father came up. Zach slid off the couch and went to his knees in front of her. Grabbing her hands with his, he locked gazes with her. "I've never regretted killing the bastard. The one thing that scares me is how I lost control of the darkness. I let it consume me. And it felt good. I don't want to become an addict of dark magic."

A tear rolled from the corner of one eye. She cupped his face and kissed his forehead. "Your heart is too pure, too caring. Use it to guide you."

Lydia's presence brushed against his subconscious a moment before the doorbell rang. "Lydia's here, and she's not alone."

After standing, he entered the foyer. That was when he heard Khloe's and Kalissa's voices. Opening the door, he frowned. "Are we having a party?"

Khloe laughed and reached out for his ear. He blocked her hand before she could touch it. With a thought, he used glamour to make his ears look human. Khloe gave him a fake pout. "I thought they were cute."

A low growl sounded right before Jagger appeared behind Khloe, Kalissa, and Lydia. "Who you calling cute?"

Khloe rolled her eyes and stepped inside the house. When Kalissa walked by Zach, she said, "Ayden and Meliana will be here shortly." Zach nodded and noticed how Lydia hung back, close to the door, holding Logan. A mix of sadness and anxiousness flowed around her.

Just then, Zach's mom and grandmother came in and greeted everyone. Once they had left, Zach stuck his hands in his pockets. "What's going on?"

Lydia met his gaze, and he grew hard. Desire ran hot in his veins, and he wanted to touch her. Kiss her. She was so beautiful to him, perfect for him. After a moment, she glanced down at Logan. "I'm binding his powers and hiding his magical signature."

Oh, man. He hated binding rituals. Hell, he'd had a few too many performed on him—at his own request. They weren't painful. Once his powers were bound, he'd just always felt like something was missing. "I don't like that you have to do that to keep him safe. But I understand why."

Lydia nodded, and her eyes watered. "I'll have to leave him here."

Without thinking, he tugged her into a hug, careful to not squeeze Logan in the process. "He'll be in good hands, and very well protected."

Relief flooded him when she leaned into him, accepting his comfort. "I know."

"After the ritual, can we go for a walk or something?"

She nodded. "Can we go to your condo? I think I need to get away from everyone afterwards."

"As you wish."

She let out a soft laugh. The slight smile brightening her features broke something inside of him. *Gods, I'm falling in love.* It was one thing to feel the pull toward his partner, but a totally different thing to realize that he couldn't ever let her go.

Lydia was his, and he was going to do whatever it took to keep her and Logan safe.

Angelica zipped the duffle bag filled with the little bits of things she owned. An uneasy feeling whirled inside her. She'd thought the need to run would lessen when she escaped Demetrius's dungeon. It hadn't. Even after all those years locked away from her family and friends, she still longed for quiet. It was odd and frightening.

Being in the Divinity House with everyone there made her anxious. Sometimes, she wanted to crawl out of her skin. Sal flew into the room and perched on her headboard. "What you doing?"

She smiled. The small, two-foot-tall dragon had become much more than just her familiar. He'd become her companion in the short time they'd been together. "Well, we are moving to the coven. Noah and Vanessa have a small cottage they said we could stay in."

"When were you going to tell everyone?"

Kris's voice rumbled through the room. She closed her eyes briefly before turning to him. He was the number one reason she wanted a place of her own. Feelings she shouldn't have, rose up and confused her. Maybe she was just lonely and thought she wanted things she couldn't have. "I just spoke to Vanessa. She offered. I planned to tell Lydia tonight."

His tiger flashed in his eyes as he prowled closer. Sal hissed and jumped to stand on her shoulder. Kris grinned. "You're a little small to be tangling with a tiger, dragon."

Sal growled but didn't move. Angelica could feel Sal's concern for her, and his hesitation, as if he were as curious as she about what Kris was about to do. Deep in her soul, she knew Kris would never harm her. He'd try to intimidate her, but not hurt her.

Kris stopped a few inches from her. "What about me?"

"I wouldn't leave without saying goodbye. However, I will only be a fifteen-minute drive or less than a second teleport away." She narrowed her gaze, studying him. When he raised his hand and gently caressed her cheek with is his fingers, her right forearm tingled.

She didn't dare look. She couldn't. It was too soon. Hell, she hadn't had a chance to mourn her husband's death. She stepped away from him and grabbed her bag. "We should go. The ritual will be starting soon."

CHAPTER NINE

"*I*'ll be here as much as possible," Lydia assured Vanessa.

The Elder witch held out her arms. When Lydia placed Logan in them, Vanessa smiled, and a tiny tear rolled from the corner of one eye. "I've missed having a baby in the house."

Cassia, Bethany's two-year-old daughter, bounced into the family room. "Logan." She rushed over and gently patted his head. "Hi."

Lydia nibbled on her bottom lip to keep a laugh in. Cassia was adorable with her long, curly, blonde hair and large, blue eyes. A moment later, Bethany entered the room with Kris and Angelica behind her. Lydia noticed the duffle bag in her mom's grasp.

Standing, Lydia moved to her mom. "What's going on?"

Dread rolled in Lydia's belly as she waited for her mom to answer. Instead, Angelica turned to the foyer. *Great, a private conversation.* Once alone—well, somewhat alone—her mom took her hand. "I feel overwhelmed in the Divinity House with everyone there."

"Is it the attack earlier? We can strengthen the wards." Panic wound around her heart. She couldn't lose her mom and son.

Angelica cupped her face, forcing her to meet her gaze. "I can tell what you're thinking by the look in your eyes. You are not losing anyone. I'll be here at the coven. Vanessa and Noah have offered me a small cottage across from the community center. I'll be here with Logan while you help the Divinities end this war."

And protect the last of her family. Lydia relaxed and tugged her mom into a hug. "You're right. I have nothing to worry about. Logan will be cared for and safe. Why do I feel like a bad mother?"

Angelica laughed softly. "You are a mother. It is our instinct to protect and care for our children. Which is what you're doing."

Her mom was right. Lydia was doing what she

could to ensure that Logan was safe and out of the demons' reach. Now she'd be free to put an end to Khan and his evil plans.

"Dia, don't be reckless."

Lydia blinked at her mom. "I'm not going in alone, don't worry."

Vanessa approached with a sleeping Logan in her arms. "Are you ready?"

Lydia nodded and followed the Elder along with Mel and the others to the basement where Noah's man cave, as Zach called it, was located. It was also where most of the private rituals were performed.

Usually, the basement was a comfortable, lounge-like room. The center of the room would be the sitting area with a sofa and chairs. Tonight, the furniture had been moved to the outer edges of the space, replaced by an altar.

Lydia followed Noah and Vanessa to the center of the room, much like she had during Jacen's passing over ceremony. But she wasn't burying anyone today. *This is for his protection.*

A moment later, Mel took her place next to Vanessa. Lydia met each of their stares briefly. "Mel said this would be temporary."

Noah nodded, his smile was gentle, and his silver-blue eyes shone with wisdom and strength.

"Yes. I wrote it so the spell would break upon Khan's death. I figured that would be for the best."

Lydia agreed, although, deep down, she panicked. What if they never killed Khan?

"Are you ready?" Mel asked softly.

"Yes. Should I hold him?"

With a short nod, Noah answered. "If you wish."

Glancing around, Lydia noted everyone in the room. Kalissa, Khloe, Ayden, Zach, Kristof, and her mother all stood in a circle around them. Each one radiated love and support. This was her family. She might have lost her dad, brother, and husband, but she'd gained so much more.

Kalissa stepped forward, placed a coal disk in the ceramic incense burner and lit it. After the coal glowed hot, she blew out the flame and then placed a pitch of frankincense on the coal. Fragrant smoke rolled out of the top of the incense burner as Kalissa moved around the circle, purifying the space.

Noah spoke in a soft but clear tone where everyone would hear him. "I'm not going to bind Logan's powers. Instead, I'm going to do a spell similar to the one I did to mask Zach's power. It's more like a dampening spell. I altered it to include a protection element. By the power of three"—he indicated himself, Vanessa, and Mel—"the spell will be unbreakable.

Lydia remained silent. Her belly was wound in knots, and she had to fight to stay in place. *"This is for the protection of your son."* Ayden's voice filtered in her mind, only giving her a little comfort. Being surrounded by empaths was worse than being bound to her telepathic brother. A new ache tightened her chest.

Jacen is one of the reasons I'm doing this. The demons would not take another loved one from her.

When she met Noah's gaze, she relaxed. Wisdom, strength, and love lit up his silver-blue eyes. She could see why the other Divinities loved him so. Being around him soothed her fears and made her believe that everything was going to be fine.

With a deep breath, she stepped closer to the trio. Each Elder kissed Logan on the forehead before joining hands, combining their powers into one ball of white energy. The room filled with an electric charge that made the hairs on Lydia's arms stand on end.

The Elders raised their arms in the air above Logan, and Noah spoke the incantation. "By Earth and Fire, we draw strength. By love and compassion, we give Logan Rayners absolute protection from

Khan and all bad intentions for all his days. Punishment will come to anyone besides his grandmother, Angelica, and mother, Lydia, who removes him from the Maxville Coven for as long as Khan lives. With the power of three, we ask the goddess Hecate to mask the young Dark Divine's powers from all with evil in their hearts so he may live safe, loved, and protected."

The electric current flowing around them intensified. A swirl of light and dark magic twirled around them, closing in until it formed a bubble around Lydia and Logan. The smell of rosemary and earth filled Lydia's senses. *Hecate*. Although the goddess didn't take physical form, she was there, granting her strength for the spell.

"Thank you, Goddess," Lydia whispered just as the bubble tightened around them, then expanded out, only to snap back a moment later. The power vanished faster than it had appeared.

Glancing down, Lydia noted a small purplish mark in the center of Logan's forehead. Noah leaned in and whispered, "Only we can see the mark. It's a warning to the demons."

She nodded. "Thank you."

Vanessa wrapped an arm around Lydia's shoulder. "Let's have some tea and cookies. And watch that sweet baby sleep."

A smile lifted Lydia's lips while an unconditional love bloomed in her heart. Family wasn't just blood. Family was everyone who would love, protect, and accept each other without question or judgment.

The one thing she'd missed while married to Mikal.

Her gaze met Zach's, and longing made her ache for his touch. Not just sexually, but to just know she belonged. They had a lot to clear up between them. Since his secret was out of the bag, it was time she confessed hers.

"Do you mind taking him? I need to talk with Zach alone." Lydia's words were soft so only Vanessa heard them.

The other witch smiled wide and nodded. "Of course."

Ayden, Noah, and Kris moved the furniture back in place while the women gathered around Logan. Lydia made her way to the stairs where Zach waited. She'd been so used to Jacen reading her thoughts growing up —not because he pried into her personal space but because he couldn't turn the telepathic ability off—she didn't mind that Zach could read her by her emotions.

Zach's empathy was comforting in a way. She welcomed it, welcomed *him*. No more running and guarding her heart. It was time to go after what she wanted.

She wanted a family and a magical mate to spend her long existence with.

Another thing she wanted was to burn Khan alive, make him pay for all the pain he'd caused the *magickin* communities. But she wasn't going to do it alone. She didn't have to. She had Zach and the Divinities.

"How do you feel?" Zach studied Lydia, unable to get a clear reading on her emotions. It wasn't because she was blocking him. She seemed to be numb.

She stopped walking and faced him. "You can't tell?"

He shrugged. "I feel numbness."

"I guess. It's more like the calm before the storm." A spark arched within her green and blue eyes as she stared at him. A moment later, she said, "What about you?"

He frowned. He'd hidden behind a spell and glamour for so long, he hadn't allowed himself to feel true emotion. The fear of losing control still haunted him. "This is where I usually say 'cool as ice.' But you know better." Taking her hand, he led her to the playground next to the community center. "I used my dark magic once before. Well, I let it use me."

Lydia tightened her fingers around his and then tugged him to sit on the merry-go-round. "It's hard for me to believe you let anything control you."

He let out a bitter laugh. "Behind the playful, sarcastic Zach you met, is darkness."

"We all have a darkness inside of us."

He raised a brow at her. "What's yours?"

She drew her brows together. "You first."

Fair enough, he guessed. "I was eight, and my dad was on one of his power-drunken binges. Usually, he would just verbally abuse my mom, but that night, he was different. He hit her, over and over. I feared he'd kill her. Bethany was at a friend's house." Zach took a deep breath, feeling the magic flowing in his blood. The thought of his bastard father touching his mom made Zach want to kill him all over again.

Lydia brought his hand to her lips. A pulse of healing power soothed away the pain he hid from everyone. He met her gaze and was lost. Papa was right. Lydia could help him. "I killed the bastard. I blasted him with a power so dark it scared me in the end. I just raised my hands and thrust all the rage and dark power I had inside at him."

"You did what you had to do to protect your mom."

He leaned into her, pressing his forehead to hers. "That's what Mom and Papa keep telling me. Bethany says I saved her from doing it."

"Was that the first time your dark elf powers showed up?"

"Yes." Like a light coming on, he realized where she was headed. "I didn't know I had that kind of power. We'd all trained in magic since we were born, like all witches. And with the Divinity bloodline running in my family, there was always a chance that one of us would develop a gift. Besides, Mom didn't know until that night that my father was a dark elf. Sure, she knew he was of elfin descent, but..."

Lydia smiled. "But she didn't know to train you to control dark magic."

Zach studied how her eyes twinkled in the moonlight. "I guess I need to stop hiding and man up."

"It's about time," she teased.

In the next moment, he was kissing her. A groan escaped him between their lips. When she threaded her fingers into his hair and tugged him closer, he grew rock-hard. The urge to teleport them to his condo was intense. The only reason he didn't, was the feeling of being needed at the coven or close to the Divinities. It was odd.

Breaking the kiss, he held her gaze. "So, what's your secret?"

Nervousness mixed with fear rushed out to him. Lydia turned to give him her profile and stared off into the night. "I...you have to understand that I've lost my husband, father, and brother all within a short period of time."

Moving to his knees, he knelt in front of her and took her hands in his. "Whatever you did, tell me. We'll move past it."

She made eye contact and breathed in, then out. When she opened her mouth, Ayden's voice entered his mind. By Lydia's wide-eyed look, she'd also gotten the message. *"There's been a demon sighting downtown. Time to rumble."*

"We'll meet you at Friendship Fountain."

Zach stood and tugged Lydia with him. Wrapping an arm around her waist, he smirked and said, "Saved by a call to go demon hunting. But don't think you'll get out of spilling your dark secret."

Then he teleported them to Friendship Fountain on the Southbank of downtown Jacksonville.

CHAPTER TEN

A bloodthirsty need to hunt fueled Lydia's desire to get to Khan and end this war. He always seemed to be a step ahead. Enough was enough.

She and Zach materialized about twenty feet from Friendship Fountain, masking their presences in case humans were around.

After making sure no one was there to witness them pop in out of thin air, they lifted the glamour that helped them hide from the humans when performing magic. Although they tried to not use too much power in public, the demons seemed to care less about exposing themselves.

Bastards.

Lydia fisted her hands at her sides. Her skin

tingled, telling her there was dark, demonic energy nearby. And it wasn't from just a few demons. "There has to be a dozen or so of them in the area."

Zach nodded beside her. "It's odd. What are they up to?"

A moment later, Ayden, Jagger, and Khloe rounded from the front side of the fountain. Khloe sniffed the air while the guys flanked her. When they reached Lydia and Zach, Khloe said, "Talk about a meeting of the ugly and stupid. What the hell? Is there a demon convention?"

Jagger growled. "They're not here."

"Is your demon sniffer broken?" Zach asked, then added, "Getting weak in your old age?"

The corners of Jagger's lips twitched, and the Death Demon flipped Zach the bird. "Okay, elf. Stretch out your senses beyond the fountain."

Lydia pressed her lips together at the taunting between the two men. Apparently, Jagger no longer saw Zach as a threat since Khloe and Jagger had mated. They'd resorted to taunts and insults over the last month.

When Zach stiffened beside her, Lydia frowned and focused on the energy. She reached out as far as it went, which was about a fifty-foot perimeter around the fountain. "It's a trap."

Suddenly, a baby's cry sliced at Lydia's heart. She followed the sound without a word to the others. The terror in the crying tore at her soul. And sounded too much like Logan. *No.* She picked up her pace and went into a jog, then a run.

Several yards down the Riverwalk, she found the baby wrapped in a bloody blanket in a basket by a dumpster. Tears rolled down her cheeks, and her hands shook as she reached for the bundle. Pulling back the blanket, she burst into tears that quickly turned to rage.

She stood and faced the others. "It's a doll and a tape recorder."

When she stepped around the others to teleport to the other side of the river and hunt down Demetrius, Zach stopped her with a hand on her upper arm. "They want you to react. It was a trap for you. Why?"

He narrowed his eyes, telling her that he suspected something. "They need to be stopped." She jerked her arm from his grasp and turned just as Samoan and two *Regals* materialized.

"Hello, huntress. I have a gift for you." The demoness thrust out a hand, and a black ball of energy flew from her palm. "You crave blood so much...now, your thirst will rule you. *Factus lamia.*"

Too late, Lydia realized that Samoan had thrown a curse at her. She twisted, but it was no use. The black ball hit her in the back, coating her, soaking into her clothes and skin. Pain burned in her gut and rapidly spread throughout her body. She was on fire.

Sinking to her knees, she gripped her head as power rushed around her. It was like being trapped in the center of a cyclone. Buzzing and sparks of heat zipping and zinging around her, through her. She screamed but wasn't sure if anyone heard her.

Lifting her head, she saw Jagger, Ayden, and Khloe fighting demons. Zach was nowhere near. Pain arched inside her head, forcing her to close her eyes.

A moment later, she felt as if someone lifted her off the ground. The world spun, and for a moment, she thought she was being dragged through jelly. When the sensation stopped, she smelled...Zach.

"Vampire." She tried to warn him, but with the humming in her ears, she couldn't tell if the word was spoken out loud.

The scent of his blood tingled her nose. The pain in her head lessened, and only then did she dare to open her eyes. Relief washed through her as she recognized Zach's room at his condo. Scanning the space, she focused on Zach coming from the bathroom with a wet washcloth.

His gaze met hers, and he frowned, his brows bunching together as his lips pursed. The thump, thump of his heart mixed with his earthy scent. She groaned as he closed the distance.

When he sat on the bed beside her, she flew—with a speed she'd never possessed before—to the other side of the room. "Stay away."

He let out a sigh. "Don't make me force you. Jagger said you need blood. Mumbled something about us being mates and that it could help you."

She shook her head while her stomach tightened and twisted with a painful hunger she was sure wasn't for food. "I'll hurt you."

"No, you won't."

"You don't know that."

Zach crawled onto the bed to kneel, facing her. "Neither do you." He stretched out a hand. "Now, come here. I'd rather your first feeding be with me than a helpless human. Or your son."

Cold fear punched her in the chest. Zach was playing dirty. Using her son to strike a nerve. It worked. She snarled. "Leave Logan out of this."

"Then come here." He tore off his shirt and tossed it to the floor. Sun-kissed, lean muscles covered his torso. The vein in his neck pulsed, and she swore she could actually hear his blood flow under his skin.

Fuck.

She pushed off the wall and stalked toward him. "What if I can't stop?"

He closed his eyes briefly. "Then I will have to... hurt you. But we are magical partners. Theory is that we can't harm each other without suffering the same pain ourselves."

He was right. However, she wasn't sure she wanted to test it.

Zach jumped forward and grabbed her hand and tugged her to the bed. Pinning her to the mattress, he smirked. "Now, bite me."

Gods, she was weak. And hungry. She struck, hard. Her fangs pierced his throat. The rush of warm, tangy blood flowed into her mouth and down her throat, soothing away the fire raging inside her.

Zach slid one arm under her and ground his hips into her core. A different kind of fire ignited, flaring into a desire for something besides his blood.

Mine.

Yes, he was hers, as she was his. She wrapped her legs around his waist, wanting to feel him. A growl rumbled from her throat. She extracted her fangs from him and snarled, "Too many clothes."

Zach stared back at her, his eyelids half closed as if he were drunk on desire. A lazy, yet seductive smile lifted his lips. "You have some explaining to do about hunting demons alone. First, I want to taste you."

Oh gods, yes. Glancing at his neck, she spotted a small stream of blood from the puncture marks. She licked the bite out of instinct, and because she couldn't let the bit of blood beading at the holes go to waste. A moment later, the small holes closed.

A smile lifted her lips while her gums ached. But before she could move to bite Zach, he nipped at her bottom lip. "It's my turn to taste you."

His tone was playful and a warning at the same time. A growl rumbled from her throat as need intensified the desire to possess him. Without warning, Zach tore her clothes from her body, exposing her to him.

A slow curve formed on his lips. "Beautiful. Fangs and all."

"You need to hurry," she warned.

He dipped his head and placed a kiss above her nipple, then swirled his tongue around the tight nub. Pleasure fired from each nerve, sending electrifying pinpricks throughout her. A moan escaped her once his teeth grazed a nipple.

Gods, it was hard to not overpower him and end the suffering he put her through with his damn teasing.

When she opened her mouth to tell Zach about it, he slid his hand down her belly and cupped her sex. *Oh.* She fisted the sheets and moved against him. The pleasure built, threatening to push her over the edge.

He pumped in and out with his fingers while rubbing his thumb over her clit. Her fangs extended again but not out of hunger. It made her wonder if the myth of vampires getting a sexual release from taking blood was true. Before she tested that out, she wanted Zach inside her.

Reaching up, she cupped the back of his head and drew him to her. Gold swirled wildly in his brown eyes. "I need you inside me, now."

One dark brow rose, but she could smell his arousal. Earth and sage mixed with rich notes of rose. She'd never noticed the complexity of his scent before. *You're a vampire now. A predator.*

A sharp sting to her earlobe brought her out of the dark thoughts. She smirked and took the opportunity to sink her teeth into Zach's shoulder. He growled out a groan and ground his jean-covered erection into her.

With a single thought, she willed his jeans gone. A moment later, he was as naked as she was.

Zach chuckled. "Someone is being naughty."

"Someone else is taking his sweet-ass time."

As soon as the last word had left her mouth, he thrust inside her. She gasped and then moaned as he moved in and out. Power wrapped around them and filled the room. Tiny pricks of electrical current nipped at her skin as she rode the wave of an orgasm, so close to the edge.

She scored Zach's back with her nails and tightened her legs around his waist. He picked up the tempo, slamming into her. Gods, he felt too good, smelled too good.

She cried out in pleasure as the climax pulled her under. Zach followed with his own release.

After the last shudder left their bodies, Zach pulled out and lay beside her, hugging her close.

She lifted her gaze to Zach's. A frown formed as reality crashed into her. She was cursed to crave blood. Although Samoan had said, "become vampire" in Latin, Lydia didn't feel any differently. At least, not now that she'd fed from Zach.

"What's wrong?" Zach traced her jawline, stopping at her chin where he rubbed his thumb across her bottom lip.

"I'm not sure. I don't feel like killing for blood anymore."

Zach laughed. "You're not craving it like a few minutes ago?"

"I'm not sure what I'm supposed to do. I mean, how often will the hunger rise?"

He kissed her quickly on the lips. "I believe you are stronger than you think. Plus, wouldn't your healing gift help you control the hunger?"

She thought about it. "It's possible."

"We can try. Also, I'll have Ayden come over in the morning so you can test your control."

Lydia frowned. She didn't like testing anything on anyone. "Could we just go hunt down some demons? I could get the whole thing out of my system and be well fed before I face anyone else."

Zach worked his jaw before answering. "From what I understand, feeding too much could put you into bloodlust. There would be no controlling the hunger once it's gone that far."

True. "I wish I knew a vampire."

He lifted on one elbow and studied her from above. His eyes narrowed. "Talking about demon hunting."

Lydia sighed. "It was the secret I was going to share with you earlier at the coven. I started hunting them down about a month after Logan was born. After seeing what the bastards did to mom, I snapped. They've taken so much from me and everyone. They need to be stopped."

His features softened slightly. "I agree with you one hundred percent. Yet, you can't go off alone. It's too dangerous. Especially with that crazy bitch Samoan on the loose."

And look at me now. Lydia groaned. "All I thought about was killing that bitch. But she got me instead."

"You could have told Khloe, and she'd have been on board with tag-teaming the demoness with you." Zach smiled and waggled his eyebrows.

"I figured you'd be mad."

Lying down beside her, he gathered her to him. His earthy scent surrounded her, soothing the worry churning in her mind. "I'm the last person to pass judgment for keeping secrets. Don't get me wrong, I don't like the fact that you went off on your own. You could've been killed."

She sighed and snuggled into him. A yawn escaped her before she spoke. "We all could be killed, even with backup."

"I know." He squeezed her closer and fell silent for a few moments before he, too, yawned. Kissing her on top of the head, he said, "Promise me no more rogue activity."

"As long as you don't hide your elfin half."

A tingle of magic rippled over him, and she glanced up to see his pointed ears and the slight glow to his skin. "You know the ears are kind of sexy."

He crinkled up his nose. "Stop teasing."

Cupping his face, she drew him close to place a long, toe-curling kiss on his lips. "I like teasing. However, on a serious note, I do like the real you."

Zach chuckled then frowned. "I'm relieved it's out in the open now. I still feel like I could lose control, though."

"Not as much as I could right now."

"We'll figure it out. The good thing is, you're cursed. And all curses can be broken." When she yawned again, he kissed her forehead and added, "Go to sleep. We can research in the morning."

Lydia nodded and closed her eyes, snuggling into him, breathing in his soothing, earthy scent. Although things looked bleak at the moment, she was sure about some things. Zach was hers. And Samoan was going to die. One day, somehow, Lydia was going to be there, waiting for the bitch.

That fucking witch was dead when Samoan got a hold of her.

Desiree had failed to report in since their little tiff a few days ago. When Samoan had told her, her son was dead. A twisted smile tugged at Samoan's lips. True, the kid his mother knew and loved *was* dead. But not the assassin Khan created. The first of the Dark Divine army.

All in due time, witches.

Samoan stalked the perimeter of the Oceanway Coven. They had strengthened the wards. To any lower-power demon, the magic weaved into the invisible shield would kill them. Not Samoan. She wasn't fully a demon. Her dark elfin half amped her demon side to levels that equaled Khan. An advantage for her in the coming mating.

The Underworld lord couldn't bully her into submission, and he knew it.

She materialized at Khan's house in the Underworld. Taking form in the great room of the gothic-style mansion, she frowned at the large vampire standing guard outside the study. The male snarled and watched her as she advanced to the door.

With a smile, she said, "Don't you have things to kill?"

A growl was her answer. She rolled her eyes and entered the study. Khan sat at an oversized black-stained oak desk, his head bent over something. Without lifting his gaze to her, he asked, "What has you so annoyed, my bride?"

"Nothing I can't handle." She dropped into a chair across from him. When he lifted his head and looked at her with a raised brow, she chuckled. "Desiree is hiding out in her coven. I'm sure she has gone to the Divinities by now."

"So, let her go to them. She'll have to reveal what a traitor she's been." Khan relaxed into his high-back throne-looking chair. His long, black hair hung loosely around his shoulders, blending into his black button-up.

He was pure evil and sexy as hell.

A wicked smile tugged at her lips. Desiree had to prove herself to the Divinities and wouldn't be a problem for Samoan. At least, for a little while. "How is Mathew?"

Khan grunted. "As stubborn as his mother. However, the kid is powerful. More so than his mom. Too bad the witch destroyed the crystal."

Fuck. Samoan had been planning to ease into that conversation. But she should have known that Khan would find out. She'd just hoped it would be later. "Yes. She lied to me about being able to charge it."

Samoan crossed her legs and bounced her foot vigorously. The Sinew was the one thing Hecate and her witches had that could stop Samoan and Khan from stopping them. If only they had one of their own... She met Khan's stare and grinned. "Make your own Sinew."

He opened his mouth, shut it, and then opened it again. His brows bunched as if he churned the idea over in his mind. "Do you know how much power it would take to create one? It was a stretch trying to charge up a dead piece of Hecate's."

Samoan uncrossed her legs and leaned forward. "You have an army of Dark Divine under your control. And the resources to take the ones who refuse. Including the *Porter* witch."

One corner of Khan's sensual mouth lifted. He flashed to stand in front of her, then knelt down. Desire bloomed within her. This was her mate. Father thought it was an arrangement. It was so much more. She and Khan were fated to be together.

When he ran his warm hands up her thighs under her black mini-skirt, she groaned. "You are brilliant. Desiree and her son will have just enough power to extract the magic from the Dark Divine."

He kissed her, making the desire turn to a wild-fire in her veins. He wrapped his arms around her and stood, taking her with him. "We must celebrate, then we hunt all the Dark Divine."

Yes. Samoan will be the one to get Desiree and torture the bitch a little before draining all her magic.

"We will get what is ours and destroy the witches for good."

CHAPTER ELEVEN

*L*ydia stretched in the king-sized bed. The sweet aroma of pumpkin mixed with the rich fragrance of coffee drifted into the room. She groaned as her belly rumbled. A smile formed at the thought of Zach in the other room. The man loved to cook. Which was fine by her.

After getting up and conjuring clothes on her body, she made her way to the kitchen. Zach stood in front of the refrigerator in nothing but jeans. She raked her gaze across his broad shoulders, then down to his trim waist. Heat flared in her belly and quickly spread throughout her body. She let out a low groan that sounded a little too much like a growl. Just then, her gums itched and her fangs lowered.

Fuck.

Alarmed, she covered her mouth with her hand and turned toward the living room, desperate to get away from him. She didn't want to feed. Not on Zach. He wasn't her personal pincushion. Damn it.

Taking deep breaths, she walked to the wall of windows overlooking the St. Johns River. The water was calm and smooth as a sheet of glass. The rising sun reflected off the surface.

After a few moments, Zach came up behind her and wrapped his arms around her. "Morning."

"Morning." The single word was gritted out. She closed her eyes, finding it almost impossible to keep from twisting in his arms and biting him.

"Don't fight it. Take from me what you need."

She shook her head. Before she spoke, the doorbell rang. When Zach released her, she whirled around, eyes wide. "I can't see anyone right now."

With a frown, he moved to the door. "I haven't called Ayden yet."

Lydia inhaled then cursed. "Shit, it's Khloe and Jagger." The desperate need to hide overwhelmed her. With inhuman speed, she darted to the hallway, only to slide to a stop when Jagger materialized in front of her.

She crouched, waiting for an attack. Zach

stepped between them and threw up a shield around her. With a low growl, he said, "Leave her alone, Jagger."

Jagger grunted as he slammed a couple of bags of blood into Zach's hand. "Give those to her. She's to have a couple of bags three times a day for the first few days, then slowly reduce it until she only needs to feed two to three times a week."

Lydia moved closer to Zach to glance over his shoulder. The label on the bag said Knight Blood Bank. Lifting her gaze back to Jagger, she frowned. "Did you steal those?"

The Death Demon threw his head back and laughed. "No. I know the owner, who happens to be the Vampire King, Kane Knight."

"Vampire King?"

Jagger gestured to the bags of blood. "Have your breakfast, and then we'll talk." Then he pushed past them to head to the living room.

Zach lowered the shield and turned to her, holding out the bags. Frowning, Lydia took them. Her fangs were still elongated from eyeing Zach in the kitchen earlier like a life-sized chocolate bar. She sighed and then punctured the bag with her fangs, surprised when they sucked up the thick liquid on their own.

After finishing the second bag, she felt better. The drive to attack someone's neck had lessened, and the slight pang in her belly was gone.

In the living room, Khloe was hooking up a laptop to the flat-screen TV mounted to the wall. Without looking at Lydia, she spoke. "We didn't mean to show up so early. I wanted to give you at least a day to get the hunger under control. But Jagger insisted you needed to know things before you turned rogue."

Lydia frowned as she lowered herself onto the cushion in the far corner of the sofa. "The only craving I have right now is to kill Samoan."

Khloe turned her head to meet Lydia's stare. A flash of white rippled through Khloe's teal gaze as her lips curled. "That makes two of us. The bitch will have her day." Picking up the remote, she clicked a button, and the TV fired up and a video conferencing app appeared, waiting for others to join the meeting. Khloe moved to the sofa and sat next to Lydia, but not too close. "Desiree showed up at Divinity House this morning."

The growl in her tone led Lydia to believe that Desiree had not been welcome, or had done something bad. "What is it?"

Jagger grunted. "The *Porter* has been a busy girl."

Lydia met Zach's gaze. The gold in his eyes brightened. "What did she do?"

"She's been working with Samoan." Khloe held a hand up to silence Zach and Lydia when they opened their mouths. "Demon bitch used Desiree's child to control her."

Desiree was a mother? Lydia stared at Khloe then glanced to Jagger, who sat in the armed chair across from them. "Desiree looks so young."

Khloe shrugged. "Apparently, *Porters* age a little slower than we do. She has a ten-year-old son. I don't know her, or what she's been through. But her emotions were so raw this morning. She's confused and in a lot of pain."

It would make sense that Khloe knew the other Divinity's emotional state. Her bond to her twin and empathic brother-in-law would allow her to read others' emotions. Plus, her inner cat gave her the ability to scent out truths and lies.

Lydia motioned to the TV. "I take it we're having a meeting."

"Yep. We're doing it this way because we believe it's better to not expose you to too many people at once." Khloe flicked her gaze to Zach then back to Lydia. "At least, until you're sure *you* are in control and not the curse."

Understanding where they were coming from didn't ease Lydia's annoyance with being a vamp. But she let it go for now. She and Zach would have to search for a way to break the curse. One thing was for sure, Lydia wasn't going to stop hunting demons.

"How did Samoan use Desiree's son?"

Khloe sighed and briefly told them about Desiree believing her son was ill and how Samoan had manipulated her into handing the boy over. "So, Lex believes that Mathew transitioned into something other than half-witch, half-*Porter*. But they don't know *what* he turned into."

Dread settled in Lydia's gut like a rock. There was no telling what Khan had planned for the boy. Or had already done to him. "Is there a rescue being planned?"

"Not until I find out it's safe to bring him over from the Underworld." Lex's voice drew Lydia's attention to the TV. It was the most Lydia had heard the Death Demon say in one sitting. She glanced at Jagger, who wore the mask of silence.

Ayden spoke next. "Lex and Desiree will handle the search and rescue for Mathew. We'll help in any way, of course. So I want to move forward with destroying the warehouse. I am concerned with computer files."

Khloe shook her head and sent Lydia a smirk. "I already got them."

"Should have known," Ayden teased before continuing. "Lex, Melaina, and I will stay here with Kalissa. You four will meet Teddy-Bear about a block from the warehouse tonight."

Khloe picked up the remote. "We'll work on a plan to set the charges."

There was an edge to Khloe's tone. Lydia studied her as she ended the video. "What's bothering you?"

"Ayden is considering moving Kalissa to the coven until after the baby is born. Maybe until after the war is over."

As a bonded sibling herself, Lydia understood how Khloe was feeling. She hadn't liked being far from Jacen when he was alive. "Then go with her. Zach and I can watch the house."

Her friend stilled and looked at her. A moment later, she dropped her shoulders and smiled. "I didn't think about that because I just couldn't see not living in the house."

"It won't be permanent. Besides, do you think Kalissa would go hide out in the coven?"

"No. She wouldn't." Khloe laughed as she closed

the distance between them and drew Lydia into a hug.

Lydia's nose tingled. With her vampire sense of smell, she picked up on the slight citrus scent of Khloe's cat. Tugging out of the embrace, Lydia wrinkled her nose. "No offense, but I don't like the way you smell."

Khloe let out another laugh. "None taken. I'll take it. It's better than you telling me I smell good enough to eat."

Jagger cleared his throat. Khloe rolled her eyes and then whispered, "His fangs are the only ones to pierce my skin."

Zach grunted. "That's a little TMI."

The playfulness between Khloe and Zach eased some of Lydia's tension. The portion that wouldn't go away was the part that worried about how Logan was doing. Her heart ached to go to him, to hug him, and to smother him with kisses. Tears stung the backs of her eyes.

A moment later, Zach wrapped an arm around her waist and handed her the phone with the other hand. "Call my grams. I'm sure your mom is there having tea."

She released a sigh and took the phone. As soon

as she did, Jagger and Khloe moved to the balcony. "Thank you."

"My pleasure." He kissed her on the forehead and then joined Khloe and Jagger.

With a heavy sigh, she dialed Vanessa's number. She answered on the second ring. "Hello, dear."

"Hi. How is he?"

Vanessa let out a breathy laugh. "Perfect. We just gave him a bath, and Angie is feeding him."

"Good." *Do not cry.* It was temporary. Plus, once she got a handle on the vamp thing, she'd be able to see him every day.

"We heard what happened. I just wanted you to know that Noah is looking for a counterspell."

Lydia's heart bloomed. "Thank you, for everything."

"Hey, we don't have to be blood to be family."

Vanessa was right on so many levels. "I'm starting to believe that now. I'll be by as soon as I can."

"I know, dear. Take care of what you need to and kick some demon ass. The sooner this comes to an end, the better." There was a slight note of envy in Vanessa's tone. Like she wished she were fighting in the war with them.

"We're working on." Lydia didn't want to give any

more information than that. After all, she wasn't a hundred percent sure they'd be able to end it anytime soon. The lingering worry that they'd walk into another trap hung heavy in the back of her mind.

Goddess help us all.

CHAPTER TWELVE

*G*etting into the warehouse was way too easy. Warning bells sounded off in her mind. The way Zach stiffly navigated the rows of shelves as they made their way to the basement door, told her he too felt it was a trap.

"I smell a trap," Bear said, not bothering to lower his voice.

Then the other hellhound head, Teddy, nodded. "Yep. It's a trap."

Just then, the pair shimmered and split apart, forming two enormous hellhounds. They were almost too big for the warehouse and definitely wouldn't fit in the basement section where the lab was located.

"Isn't it safer if you two are together?"

Teddy puffed out his body, trying to be more intimidating than he was, which was freaking scary as hell to most. "Technically, yes. But we fight better apart, as a team."

"Teddy's right. Plus, our priority is to keep all of you safe."

Khloe let out a soft growl. "You two talk loud enough to wake the dead."

Together the hounds said, "They already know we're here."

Just then, the doors to the loading docks, and the front door blew open. A dozen or so demons rushed inside. Lydia opened her senses and magic to the fire element, ready to light up a few demons.

When they charged straight for the hounds, Lydia's gut burned with dread. "They're after Teddy-Bear."

"On it," Zach said as he barreled toward the demons.

As Lydia followed suit, Khloe and Jagger were causing their own distraction. The hounds could take on a few or so demons, but not a dozen *Regals*.

One of the hounds yelped, and Lydia growled. She threw a fireball the size of a large exercise ball at two of the demons. Once it made contact, they screamed and twisted to glare at her. A moment later, the fire extinguished. What the fuck?

"Nothing I use on them is working," Khloe shouted before she cried out in pain.

Lydia turned in time to see a very pissed off Khloe shift into a large black jaguar, teeth bared. She roared then charged at the demon who'd hurt her, latching her jaw onto his neck. With a quick jerk of her head, the demon went limp.

A moment later, pain exploded on Lydia's knee and then raced up the nerve that to her spine. Lydia growled and whirled around, her fangs extended. The demon raised a brow. "Nice, a Divinity with fangs."

"All the better to rip your throat out." She rushed forward, slamming into the demon. They fell to the floor and rolled. Lydia snapped her teeth and then smiled wickedly when she made skin contact. With her hand wrapped around his throat, she called her healer's gift and gave the bastard everything she had.

The *thump, thump* of the demon's heart slowed. Her vamp senses amped her Divinity power, and she could actually visualize his heart in her mind. She imagined her hand around the organ and squeezed. The demon coughed, then stilled.

Something in her subconscious pinged, followed

by a sharp pain in her chest, and made her whip her head up. "No!" She scrambled to her feet and ran to Zach.

There was a demon with a sword raised over his head while he fought off another. A moment before she reached him, Zach's glamour fell away, and he threw out his hands. A grey cloud of energy surrounded him, then shot out, expanding in a circle. Much too late, she realized she was in the path. Once his spell, or whatever it was touched her, she seized and dropped to the ground.

No. This couldn't happen. They were magical partners, unable to harm each other. Her vision blurred, and it was hard to stay awake. Right before she lost consciousness, she heard Jagger say something about the vampire curse.

"Lydia!"

Zach's heart stopped the moment she dropped to the floor. His pulse returned in an erratic beat as he rushed to her.

"The vampire curse made her part demon. Your spell was directed at the demons." Jagger squatted next to him.

Zach grunted, not needing the male so close to *his* mate. "We're not supposed to be able to harm each other."

A moment later, Khloe, still in cat form, came over and sat on Zach's other side. She let out a soft whine as she looked down at Lydia. Zach expected a smartass remark from the hellhounds. When he didn't hear it, he glanced up and scanned the area.

They were gone.

Jagger growled. "Lex and I will stir up the *Lackey* communities. We'll find out where they took Teddy-Bear."

Zach lifted Lydia in his arms and teleported to his grandfather's study. He was glad Papa was the only one there when he materialized.

With brows drawn, Noah asked, "What happened?"

"I happened," Zach said dryly. "The first time I use my elfin power and I kill my own mate."

Noah tsked and pointed at the couch. "Lay her down." When Zach did as he was told, Noah hovered a hand over Lydia's forehead then down her body. "She's not dead, just stunned. What spell did you use?"

"Not sure, really. I heard Lydia scream, and the demons were everywhere. I focused on them and willed them gone." Zach sank onto the couch at Lydia's feet. As he removed her boots, a thought came to mind. "Oh, no."

"What?"

"I willed all the demons gone. I wasn't specific. That would have included Teddy-Bear."

Noah sighed and walked to his altar. "It's fixable. I have some incense that can wake Lydia. I'm guessing the hounds are in the Underworld."

On the heels of Papa's words, Zach sent Ayden a telepathic message about the hounds. His reply was, *"I'll let Lex and Jagger know."*

Noah came over and handed him an incense burner and a lighter. "When she wakes, she'll want to feed. I'll be upstairs if you need me."

Zach nodded and waited for Noah to leave the basement before lighting the coal under the herbal mixture. After the incense had started to smoke, he waved the holder over Lydia and then set it on the coffee table. A few long moments passed before she started to stir.

When she opened her eyes and glared at him in confusion, he said, "I thought I killed you."

CHAPTER THIRTEEN

*L*ydia blinked at Zach's sad, regretful tone. His usual earthy scent had a hint of soured fruit. Must be what sadness smelled like. She frowned. Almost twenty-four hours of being cursed, and she was adapting quite well. What did that mean?

Pushing the question aside, she sat up and cupped Zach's cheek. "To be honest, so did I." When he moved away from her, she gripped his arm and tugged him back to her. "But you didn't. *And*, you didn't mean to. In fact, you saved us all."

He shook his head, and dread hit her in the chest. "Who?"

"Teddy-Bear. I accidentally sent them with the demons."

She hugged him tightly, which caused them to roll off the couch and onto the floor. "We'll get them back. We'll just go get them."

Zach stared at her from above her. The sour notes in his scent disappeared. Flicking her gaze to his throat, she groaned softly at the sound of his blood flowing in his veins. He leaned down and brushed his lips against hers. "Take what you need. Hell, be as rough as you want. I deserve it."

She nipped his lips with her fang and licked the warm, coppery liquid. "I'll take from you, but you don't deserve punishment." When he opened his mouth to speak, she placed a finger over his lips. "Hush. No arguing with me."

"Yes, ma'am." He lifted one side of his mouth.

She cupped the back of his head and drew him in, then turned his head to the side and bit down. The flow of his warm blood touching her tongue and then sliding down her throat stirred desire she'd never felt before. Being a vampire had its advantages.

His pleasure instantly washed over her, mixing with her own. As soon as he tightened his arms, the world around them dissolved, replaced by Zach's bedroom a moment later. But it wasn't the one at the condo. Scenting the air, she realized they were still in the Daniels' house.

"What?"

She met his stare, smirked, hooked a leg around him, and flipped them over so she straddled his waist. "Just thinking of all the ways to fuck you."

"Really? Do share." He tucked his hands behind his head and raised a brow in challenge.

Challenge met. She used her magic to strip them of their clothes, then climbed down his body, nipping at his skin along the way. "You should know me enough by now not to challenge me."

He smiled, wide and brilliant. It made him look more handsome than ever. She'd have to remember to make him smile like that more often.

She curled her fingers around his cock and slowly stroked. A sharp intake of breath sent a jolt of satisfaction through her.

She took him in her mouth and sucked.

Zach jerked his hips. "Fuck." The word was a growled whisper.

Smiling, Lydia continued the slow strokes with her tongue as she sucked him and allowed her fangs to graze him. His thigh muscles under her hands flexed and then tightened as if he were fighting to gain control. Good.

She glanced up, and their eyes locked. The gold in his eyes dominated the rest, glowing. She could command anything of him in that moment.

His balls tightened, and he spoke her name in warning. Releasing him from her mouth, she climbed his body and settled her pussy over his impossibly hard cock. Before she could lower herself onto him, he gripped her hips and thrust up inside her.

Pleasure exploded within, and she almost climaxed at the feel of him so deep. Oh, gods. Sex with Zach got better each time. Or was it the blood bond strengthening their magical one? She didn't care.

She wanted him. Right then, and always.

Pleasure mounted, pushing her closer to climax. She rode him, harder, meeting each thrust until she couldn't hold on anymore. An orgasm tore through her, and she had to stifle a scream to keep the others from hearing them.

Zach gritted his teeth as his own climax peaked.

She lay on his chest and listened to his rapid heartbeat. With deep breaths, she tried to calm her own rapid pulse. In that moment, she didn't want to leave the room or deal with the demons. She was where she belonged.

In Zach's arms.

Zach hugged Lydia close, loving that he felt so connected to her. It was as if they were bonding much more than just the Divinities bond.

"I think by taking your blood, I've bound myself to you."

Her words echoed his thoughts. Breathing in her scent, he kissed the top of her head. "Are you okay with that?"

She lifted her gaze to his. "Only if you are."

"I've wanted you from the night we met. You've been through so much...I will wait." He meant it, too. She was his. He wasn't ready to admit it a few days ago, but now he knew he couldn't let her go. At least not without a fight.

She crawled up his body and gave him a quick kiss. "I wasn't sure I wanted to love another. Didn't think I had it in me."

Her eyes grew round just as his heart skipped a few beats. "What are you saying?"

She nibbled on her bottom lip before speaking. "I...um...I'm falling in love with you."

Framing her face, he kissed her. Instantly, she opened and tangled her tongue with his. Breaking the kiss, he gazed into her blue and green eyes. "I'm falling hard."

She frowned and made small circles on his chest. "What if I want to stay a vampire?"

"I'm cool with it. I mean, it comes with some pretty good perks." He waggled his eyebrows, which made her laugh. Then he asked, "Why do you ask?"

She shrugged. "I guess I'm getting used to it, seeing the perks. My Divinity gift is amped, along with the rest of my magic. Plus, I know it seems too early, but I think I'm in control of my hunger."

"Really? I'm not surprised. You are a strong person with a strong will."

"Or just too damned stubborn."

"Well, I wasn't going to say it out loud."

Lydia slapped at him. "You don't have to agree." She smiled widely. Her fangs weren't elongated, but he could see their points. "As I was saying. When I woke up in the basement, I could smell everyone in the house, knew exactly where they were. But I only wanted your blood."

A smile lifted his lips. "Because I have premium blood."

She laughed and then bit his pec, not breaking the skin. "Don't get a big head."

"Oh, I got one."

"Zach!"

He laughed and flipped her to her back, her skin pressed against the cool satin sheets. Her laugh reached her eyes and made them twinkle with life and happiness. For the first time in his life, he was comfortable and truly happy. "I love you."

The words tumbled out before he realized what he was saying. Lydia stared wide-eyed for a brief moment and then fumbled over her words. He pressed a finger to her lips. "You don't have to say the words. I just want you to know. I've never been so relaxed around anyone. Hey, you even like my pointed ears."

She relaxed. "I do like your ears." It was several moments of them staring at each other before she spoke again. "You know what?"

"What?"

She lifted her head and nipped at his chin. "I want to see your bike."

"I've got a better idea. I'll borrow Papa's bike, and then we'll go get yours." Her face brightened.

"I'd love to go for a ride."

He would, too. And to share the thrill with Lydia meant more than anyone could ever know. She might not be ready to say the words, to admit to herself that she loved him, he already knew. The link between them grew each time she took his blood told him. Plus he was an empath. She couldn't hide her feelings from him.

CHAPTER FOURTEEN

*L*ydia and Zach pulled up to the Divinity House at 6:00 AM. They'd ridden all night. Well, they'd stopped a few times to take in the clear, crisp, fall night. She loved being with him, sharing her secrets and her life with him.

Even though she'd loved Mikal, they weren't magical partners like she and Zach. There was no denying that they were meant to be together.

Just as she dismounted from her bike, the front door of the house flew open, and Khloe rushed out dressed in a pink babydoll nightie. Her blonde and pink hair was a ruffled mess around her face and shoulders. "We had a vision. I mean, Kalissa had a vision." She rubbed her eyes. "It's too fucking early. I need coffee." She turned around and went back inside.

She sent a curious glance to Zach, who shrugged. Together, they mounted the stairs and were met by Kalissa at the door. A frown marred her face, and the fragrance of worry and fear clung to her skin. "Sindee was taken by demons. They are still collecting the Dark Divine."

Ayden appeared behind Kalissa and wrapped his arms around her. "Come inside." He paused and studied Lydia. "You good?"

Nodding, Lydia tamped down the slight hurt that bloomed in her heart. She understood his concern. "Yes. It's weird. I'd expect to be a raving loon when around others."

"I'm not surprised. You have a very strong will." Ayden gave a short nod to Zach and stepped aside.

Five minutes later, they were piled in the living room. Khloe was working on her second cup of coffee and had changed into a pair of jeans and a pink t-shirt. Kalissa sat in Ayden's lap in the armchair next to the fireplace, which had a fire going.

Mel joined them a few moments later and sat on the couch next to Khloe. The house seemed a little empty without Lydia's mom and uncle. Maybe it was just that she missed them. She'd have to stop by and see them. Although, she'd been there last night and hadn't dared to go see them.

Bloodlust may not control her, but she was beginning to crave blood again. Retreating to the window closest to the front door. It slid open a few inches, and Lydia darted her gaze to Mel. The telepathic Divinity Elder smiled. Lydia mouthed, "Thank you."

A moment later, Jagger and Lex walked through the door. Jagger handed her a couple of bags of blood. Lex moved to stand in his usual spot next to the stairs and closer to the back door. She wondered what Lex's story was. Why was he so distant from everyone?

He had a lethally calm edge to him. His energy said to fuck off, which would make humans just stay out of his way. However, there was pain hidden deep inside him.

"*Stop reading me, vampire.*" Lex held her stare. There was a slight tease to his telepathic tone.

She pressed her lips together to hide a smile and sent a thought back, "*Just call it a healer's instinct.*"

Willing her fangs to lower, she popped a bag of blood to them while Ayden began the meeting.

"Teddy-Bear is missing, and now more of the

Dark Divine are disappearing. Kalissa called Sindee at the law office this morning, and when she didn't get an answer, she called her assistant. Sindee didn't show up for work yesterday. And hasn't called." Ayden let out a sigh and rubbed circles on Kalissa's back. "We know Khan wants to make an evil version of the Sinew. But why bother when he has TB?"

"Wait," Khloe spoke up, "Do the hounds have the Sinew on them? I thought they sent it to a secret hiding spot when they fought with us."

Zach nodded. "I'm hoping that is the case. We still have to go get them."

"It's not your fault they're there." Ayden studied Zach for a moment.

Jagger gave Zach a nod and met Lydia's stare. "The demons were commanded to take the hounds. Samoan got to Ryn and tortured him until he spilled everything he knew."

Lydia's chest tightened. "Is he…?"

Lex growled. "He's alive and safe for now."

Relief eased some of her tension. Even though she felt Ryn was off at times, she wouldn't wish him harm. "Samoan needs to be stopped."

"The bitch needs to die," Khloe added with a growl.

Mel nodded. "At least she needs to be knocked

off her throne and made to feel a fraction of the pain we've felt at her hand."

Yeah, take something from her. Make her suffer. "Kill Demetrius."

"I'm game." Khloe held up a hand and grinned from ear to ear.

Ayden shook his head. "We can't just go in and kill him. Good gods, what is wrong with you people?"

"Human laws don't apply to Demetrius." Zach ran a hand through his hair. "Just because we pledged a vow to uphold the laws and protect the humans... This is different. The demon needs to be taken out so we can focus on Khan."

Ayden rubbed the back of his neck then pressed his forehead to Kalissa's shoulder. "What do you propose?"

"Lydia and I can go in. Today. He'd never expect a daytime attack."

Lydia shot a glance to Zach. He was serious, and his dark elf half was showing. The war had gone on long enough. "With Demetrius out of the picture, we can work on taking out Khan. Samoan will be grieving and off her game."

"Fine." Ayden Glanced over his shoulder to Lydia. "Use your curse to your advantage."

"I plan to." She met Lex's stare. "When do you leave for the Underworld?"

"We'll leave at sunset."

Lydia nodded. She was going to bring Teddy-Bear back and help search for Sindee. But she was also going to face Samoan after the demoness realized her dear ol' dad was dead. The bitch was going to wish she'd never cursed Lydia.

Zach and Lydia crept along the backside of Demetrius's warehouse. The business looked closed. No one came in and out of the loading docks or the front doors. Then again, Demetrius used the warehouse for more demonic activities. Ones Zach and the others weren't quite sure about. They didn't know what went on.

"Do you think Khan gave Demetrius this warehouse gig to keep him busy?"

Lydia laughed. "I think so. But he is living on this side so he'd need money to live, too."

Why did she have to be so serious? Moving closer to her, he whispered, "That too, but seriously, what does he do for Khan?"

"Besides be a pain in the ass?" Lydia smiled and then nodded to the door. "There are two *Lackeys* standing guard on the other side of that door."

The corner of his mouth lifted. Khloe had dug into the business records, and from what she could tell, no humans worked inside the warehouse. And if they did, they were most likely shells anyway. Their free will stolen by the *Regals*, turning them into slaves.

They would be better off dead. Once the humans' minds had been wiped and controlled to the extremes Demetrius took them, there was no coming back from it.

"You ready?" Lydia asked.

"Yep. Let's do this."

With her vampire super-speed, Lydia zipped to the doors and ripped them open. The *Lackey* guards whirled around but didn't have time to react before Lydia twisted both of their necks. Then she dropped their bodies like a sack of potatoes.

Damn, she's hot. On the heels of that thought, her

head snapped in his direction, and she narrowed her eyes. Then a slow, sensual smile formed on her lips. Desire rolled from her, but it wasn't purely sexual. She was in hunting mode. "Demetrius is here."

Then she darted off to the back of the building, hunting down her prey. Zach let out a soft curse and followed. A vampire on the hunt was dangerous to her and those around her. It was a good thing no one else had come with them.

Lydia disappeared behind a door in the far corner of the warehouse. A moment later, Zach entered the same room and skidded to a halt. Two *Regals* and Demetrius stood over Lydia as she knelt on her hands and knees, fighting to breathe. Zach's heart stopped for a beat and then kicked up when rage shot through his veins. Dark magic was alive deep inside him.

Demetrius would pay for harming his mate.

Raising his right hand, he pointed at Demetrius. Power flowed to his fingertips, causing a blueish glow that spread to cover his whole hand. "You of all people should know not to mess with one's mate."

Demetrius's eyes darkened as he narrowed them. Zach opened his empathy and searched the demon. Pain, heartache, and rage stood guard over all other emotions. He'd lost a love. Samoan's mother perhaps.

Zach really didn't care. "Was it a witch who stole your mate?'

A twitch formed in his temple. *Ah. Struck a nerve.* "Demetrius waved a hand, and the *Regals* charged forward. Zach thrust his hand out, shooting a stream of energy at the demons. The blast hit them both, sending them flying cross the room. They crashed into the wall and crumbled to the floor.

They would only be stunned for a few moments so Zach shot out his other hand, using Demetrius's surprise to his advantage.

Just as the blast hit the demon, Lydia reached up and grabbed his leg in an iron grip. Demetrius roared as flames covered his body.

When Lydia released Demetrius, Zach went to her and drew her into his arms. "Are you okay?"

She nodded. "Take me out of here."

She didn't have to ask him twice. He teleported them to his riverfront condo. The need to have her close and make sure she was okay fueled the need to search every inch of her naked body.

CHAPTER FIFTEEN

"For the last time, Zach, I'm fine." Lydia moved her hips against his, drawing a moan from him.

With a low, growl-like sound, he met her gaze. "What happened?"

She sighed. "They must have known the moment we entered the warehouse because they were ready. My thirst for his blood and death made me careless. I was too lost in the hunt."

"Well, that was our focus, and the point of going there." Zach kissed her forehead. Fatigue started to settle over him. He'd used up a lot of power in the warehouse, more than he had since the night he'd killed his father.

Lydia cupped his face in her hands, forcing him

to meet her gaze. She gave a warm, sexy smile and drew his face to hers. When their lips touched, a warm flow of magic sparked between them. The magic filled Zach, energizing and strengthening. Gathering up the energy, he pushed it back into Lydia.

She groaned and moved against him. In the next moment, they were naked, and Lydia cupped him, rolling his balls as she rubbed. Desire fueled the magic, intensifying the power exchange between them. If she didn't stop, he'd come any minute.

Gripping her wrist, he pinned her arm over her head. She smiled, showing the tips of her fangs. Fuck, if he didn't get harder.

She took that opportunity to push the power back into him. He gasped as it hit him suddenly, zinging off each nerve. Damn. The rush of magic felt too good, blending with his dark side.

Staring down at her, he pushed his hips forward, entering her as he returned the power. She arched her back and screamed out in pleasure; her orgasm washing over him like his own. That was when he realized they were fully connected. By magic, body, and soul.

When Lydia came down from the climax, she pushed another wave of energy into him. This one hit him harder. He roared and thrust deeper inside her, feeling her milk him and bring him to his own release.

After pulling out, he fell to his side next to her and drew her close. "I think we just completed the bond."

"Yep." She snuggled into him.

"You're okay with that?"

She lifted her gaze. The blue and green coloring of her eyes glowed and swirled together from the leftover magic running in their veins. "Yes. I thought I could hold off, give myself time to adjust and help end this war before committing. But I can't deny that I'm in love with you."

His chest tightened, and his heart expanded. "I love you, too."

She kissed him quickly on the lips before saying, "We can't celebrate until we get Teddy-Bear back and end this war."

"Let's get a shower and head over to the Divinity House. I'm sure Samoan won't wait to avenge her father's death." He hoped the demoness hadn't already gathered an army.

Samoan had just entered Khan's chambers when it hit her. Like being punched in the gut, she gasped, and her heart clenched. An achy tightness she hadn't felt since the day her mother died threatened to consume her; pull her into the dark void of nothingness.

Father.

No. She started to shake. He was gone. She felt it deep in her soul. The small thread that had connected them from her birth was severed.

Khan appeared in front her and cupped her face. A tenderness she hadn't expected sparked in his dark gaze. "They will pay for this."

She nodded, not surprised that he knew. Maybe she'd spoken her pain out loud, or their growing bond was stronger than she'd realized. She may have threatened to kill her father many times, waiting for the day he'd betray her, but that was different. "This ends."

A wicked half smile lifted her lover's lips. "You have a plan?"

"We attack the Maxville Coven, take out everyone they love. Then, when they come running, we get them while they're down." Rage brewed inside her, making it hard to focus and stay put.

"I have a better idea." Khan's cool, silky voice calmed her a little. "We have the hounds, so we wait for them to come and get them. Let them come to us. In our realm."

A slow smile curved her lips. Yes, they will want their precious hounds back. "We'll have them right where we want them. Plus, we can introduce them to your new army."

Snaking his arms around her, Khan jerked her body flush with his. "We have much planning to do."

"Yes." Desire heated her from the inside. The glow of power in Khan's gaze made her needy for more. More of him. She threaded her fingers through his long, black hair and nipped at his lips. "Tell me all about how we're going to destroy the Divinities as you fuck me."

He chuckled and pressed his hard, fabric-covered length against her. The barrier of their clothes annoyed the hell out of her, so she willed them away. *Ah, that's better.* She groaned at the skin-to-skin contact and the feel of his cock brushing her.

Taking him in her hand, she pumped. His moan was music to her ears.

"The witches will not die a quick death." He plunged two fingers inside her.

"Yes." The Divinities would pay for everything they'd done. They wouldn't get away with messing with Samoan's family. She was going to enjoy torturing each one.

CHAPTER SIXTEEN

*T*hey'd arrived at the Divinity House an hour ago, and Zach was already ready to run out the door screaming. The emotions and tension in the house seeped through the wall he'd thrown up to block his empathy.

"So we go in, expecting to walk into a trap. Did you really think Samoan wouldn't know the moment her father died?" Lydia crossed her arms and worked her jaw.

Kalissa had had another vision. However, this one didn't make much sense, and she was still trying to decipher it with Ayden. Usually, when a Divinity was pregnant, their Divine gifts were limited. But Kalissa's visions had been firing off almost regularly in recent weeks.

"The demons are restless, and there was a clear attack in the vision. I just don't know if it's the past or the future. Or maybe history repeating itself." Kalissa hugged her belly.

Ayden cradled his mate close. "I'm taking Kalissa to Noah and Vanessa's. With me, Kris, and Angelica at the coven, Noah has backup in case of an attack there. Mel, Khloe, and Jagger will be here."

Desiree spoke softly from the back of the living room. "Mom and a few of the Dark Divine have the Oceanway Coven secure. We sent out a bulletin on Magical Enchantment."

Lex materialized next to the stairs. "The demons are on high alert in the Underworld. Word is buzzing about Demetrius's death."

"Now is the best time to go in, before Samoan gathers an army." Zach ran a hand through his hair.

With a nod, Lex turned to the back door. Zach, Lydia, and Desiree followed. Once outside, Zach glanced to the barn and an ache formed in his chest. It was strange not having Teddy-Bear pop their large heads out and make some kind of smartass comment or point out the obvious. *We're coming for you guys.*

Lex faced him, Lydia, and Desiree and then exposed the amulet he wore around his neck. "*Apertus.*" The single word of Latin seemed to boom through the night air. A moment later, a large oval-shaped portal appeared and opened. "This opens up to my backyard in the Underworld. Your presences will be felt. The demons in the Underworld blame the witches for trapping them there."

Yep, Zach knew the history. The war between the demons and witches had existed since the dawn of time. Or so it seemed. It had been a group of witches who banished the demons to the Underworld.

They stepped through the portal into a dim, almost colorless place. There were no firepits in this section of the Underworld. However, the magic drifting on the air was heavy like an invisible layer of fog.

"I bet there are no fairies here," Zach muttered.

Lydia added, "If there are, they're mean as hell."

Lex was the last one to walk through the portal so he could close it behind him. Then he grabbed Desiree's hand and moved past them without a word, leaving Zach and Lydia to follow.

Once inside the large, two-story home, Zach led Lydia to the open living room while Lex disappeared down the hallway. Desiree hung out by the kitchen island, wringing her hands. Sadness and anger mixed with her need to find her son.

"This isn't her fault," Lydia whispered to him.

He nodded and then spoke to Desiree. "We don't blame you."

She glanced at them and frowned. "All the power I have, and I couldn't detect a demon when I really needed to."

Lydia grunted. "Samoan isn't a full demon. She fooled all of us."

Desiree shrugged. "I guess."

They fell silent for a few moments before Desiree changed the subject. "Lex says this used to be Hecate's house before Khan took over."

Zach nodded. He could feel the goddess's magical signature lingering in the air. He wandered if she came here to visit. "I can feel her here. It's empowering. Like she's with us."

"Because she is," Lex said as he entered the living room with an armful of rolled maps. "She can't enter this realm anymore. Khan banned her from it when she refused to help him tear down the veils to the three worlds. But she can be here in spirit."

He pointed to a large onyx sphere on the top shelf of the bookcase to their right. Zach studied it for a few moments. Magic swirled around it, protecting it. "Is it risky to have it here?"

"No. It holds no magic. It's just a link to her. And the only way she can enter this realm if she has to."

Something is the Death Demon's tone left a sour taste in Zach's mouth.

"And what happens if she has to?"

"The punishment for breaking the banishing spell is death."

Lydia sucked in a breath, and Zach closed his hand around hers. Hecate loved her witches and her other children. She'd sacrifice herself to protect them.

Lex rolled out two of the maps on the small, round table in the middle of the room. "There are no cell phones or Wi-Fi down here. Khan has cut all types of communications to the natural world. So we'll do this old school."

Desiree stepped closer to the table as Lex started explaining the layout. "Khan's castle is there." He pointed to a spot at the foothill of a mountain. "We are here." He placed a finger on an area not far from the castle.

"Close, then. What about security?"

Lex smirked and pulled out the second map from under the first. It wasn't a map. It was the blueprints of Khan's castle. "Jagger stole these after our village was attached. He wasn't sure at the time why, but he said we'd need them."

"Nice," Lydia breathed

LIA DAVIS

Desiree leaned in for a closer look. "Where would Matty be?"

Zach narrowed his eyes at Desiree and opened his empathy. She wasn't being selfish. Her heart was broken over her missing son. His safety was at the forefront of her mind. Beside him, Lydia fisted her hands. Before she could lash out at Desiree, Zach covered her hand. "It depends on Khan's end game. That will determine where any of our loved ones are housed."

Lifting her gaze, Desiree frowned, and tears filled her eyes. "I'm sorry. I didn't mean to sound…"

When Zach reached out to comfort her, Lex let out a warning growl. Zach lowered his hand and stared at the Death Demon. "You know I'm mated."

Lex pointed to a spot on the blueprint. "The entrance is here. But we'll go in here." He moved to a spot at the backside of the castle. "It's not on here, but there is a hidden entrance. Ryn told me about it."

"How is he?" Lydia asked.

"Recovering. Hecate is taking care of him." Lex worked his jaw then rolled up the blueprint and map. "The sooner we head out, the better."

They all nodded and waited for Lex to lead the way.

"I have a feeling this isn't just going to be a trap." Lydia's tone hovered between gloom and giddiness.

Lex returned to the room after putting the maps up. "It'll be a full-on attack once they discover we're inside."

"A bloodbath," Desiree added.

Lydia's senses were on full alert. She heard every sound, scented every new smell. The castle was crawling with *Regals*. And there were Dark Divine within the walls somewhere. "I can't pick up the hounds' scent."

"They're here," Lex said with a growl. "They're separated and masked with a spell."

Lydia's gut twisted. Being apart for so long would weaken them. One or both could go insane from not having the contact with each other. "Do you know where they are?"

Lex gave a short nod and darted down a hallway

in the lower level of the castle. She and Desiree followed. Zach took the tail to look out for demons from behind.

"Things are too quiet." Zach spoke in a hushed tone, but Lydia could feel his concern and fear for what was ahead of them.

A few feet down the hall, Lex stopped and faced them. Gesturing to a door they'd stopped a few feet from, he said, "Teddy is in there. Zach and Lydia, get him. Desiree and I will get Bear. We'll meet back at the Divinity House."

Before Lydia could ask any questions, Lex gripped Desiree's arm and disappeared down the hall. Glancing at Zach, Lydia said, "He knows something."

"Yeah. But he is right about getting the hounds and getting out. This is too risky. I itch all over." He surveyed their surroundings and then motioned to the door. "After you."

Pursing her lips, she gripped the doorknob and opened the door. The room was dark, but with her new night vision, she could see well enough. Plus, she could hear Teddy's shallow breathing. Her heart sank, and she rushed to the large cage in the middle of the room.

She conjured a lantern and lit it. The light of the

small flame bathed the area in a soft glow.

Teddy lifted his head. "Bear?"

Lydia reached through the bars and stroked his head. "Lex and Desiree are going to get him and meet us at home."

Focusing on her healing power, she scanned Teddy for injuries. When she didn't find any, she healed his soul and heart. The two things that started to fail when he was separated from his twin. His body glowed from the inside.

He let out a soft groan. After a few moments, he stood and snarled. "Let's blow this food truck."

He teleported from inside his cage to the outside, then stretched. "Oh, that's better." His ears perked up at the same time Lydia heard at least a dozen or so pairs of boots pounding against the concrete floor, echoing down the hall.

Teddy and Lydia locked gazes and said at the same time, "We need to move."

The three of them rushed out the door and down the hall, in the opposite direction the demons were coming from. When they reached the end of the corridor, Teddy stopped and listened. Lydia stretched out her senses but didn't pick up on anything different.

A moment later, Bear barreled around the

corner. The hounds butted heads and then merged into their two-headed, ten-foot-tall hellhound form. Bear announced, "Lex and Des are right behind me. There's a bomb."

In the next moment, Bear and Teddy said the incantation to open a portal. When the doorway opened, the hounds pushed Lydia and Zach through then jumped in themselves, slamming it closed behind them.

Several minutes ticked by, and still no Lex and Desiree. "Where are they? How much time did they have?"

Lydia's heart raced, and she started to pace. When Jagger came out onto the porch, he said, "Lex is alive but not coming here."

Zach whirled around. "Why? What happened?"

Jagger worked his jaw. "I don't know. He won't tell me anything else."

Just then, Zach's cell phone rang. He answered it and put it on speaker, not that Lydia needed him to. "Yeah."

Ayden let out a relieved breath before dropping a shit-ton bomb on him. "The attack Kalissa saw earlier is happening in the next few moments. Somehow, the portals are opening. Get the hell out of the house."

Lydia gasped, and then Jagger added, "Khloe and Kalissa's parents didn't live at the coven because they were protecting one of the portals. At the farm."

Damn it. Lydia glanced around. "So, any minute now, demons are going to invade this realm, and we're standing on one of the landing pads. Fuck."

Zach echoed her curse. "Can't we close it or seal it or something?"

"You can't, but we can."

They turned to Teddy-Bear, and standing beside them was Hecate, holding the Sinew. She nodded to Zach and Lydia. "I'll need your help. With the power of three, plus the Sinew, we can close all seven portals around the world."

Zach shook his head. "Me? Why? I'm not a Divinity."

"No, but you are an elf with great power who is mated to a Divinity."

Lydia watched Zach process the goddess's words. When he didn't look convinced, she took Zach's hand and tugged him over to Hecate. "Guide us through what needs to be done."

"We will link hands and open ourselves to our power as well as that of the Sinew." When Zach still didn't look convinced, the goddess placed a hand on his shoulder. "Your dark power is what I need to close the portals. It's never controlled you. Your magic does exactly what you will it to do."

He stared at her and smiled. "And everything happens for a reason." He straightened his spine and tightened his hold on Lydia's hand. "I'm ready. Use and abuse me, my goddess."

Hecate closed her eyes briefly. A slight twitch of his lips told Lydia she was trying not to be amused by Zach. When she opened her eyes again, she held out her hands. Lydia and Zach each took one and then linked hands with each other to form a small circle.

Teddy-Bear moved in behind the goddess and placed the Sinew around her neck. The sphere instantly started to glow. A steady stream of power flowed from Hecate, filling Lydia with magic so strong and pure that she felt as if she could fly and kill a thousand demons in one fell swoop.

"Focus on the purity of the magic and direct it to the portals. It doesn't matter that you don't know where they are, just visualize one of them and will them all locked." Hecate's words were calming, and her tone made Lydia believe they could do this.

Closing her eyes, Lydia focused on the portal close by while Hecate chanted. "Seven portals around the world hear us, obey us. Closed and no more open without the key, the Sinew. Hear us and obey us."

Lydia and Zach started chanting with the goddess, saying the words over and over. Magic charged the air around them, pricking her skin and rushing through her hair. Whispers of evil swirled around her head. Lydia pushed them away and focused on shoving the negativity through the portals right before they slammed shut.

A moment later, the magic inside their circle expanded, growing stronger and larger. They chanted louder and raised their linked hands.

Then Hecate yelled, "We will it so, so shall it be!"

The power snapped outward like a rubber band, breaking their connection. Lydia flew backwards and landed on her ass a few feet away from where they'd stood. Glancing at the others, she noted they'd gotten thrown back, as well.

"It is done," Hecate said and sagged.

The hounds went to her and nuzzled her. She reached up and petted both heads. "Come. You can recharge with me in the Afterworld."

Then they dematerialized.

Zach crawled to Lydia and hugged her tightly. "How are you feeling?"

"Good. You?"

"Good."

They sat in the grass, holding each other for several long moments. Finally, Lydia stood and held out her hand. Zach took it. When he stood, she noticed a slip of paper on the ground where Hecate had sat. Odd. It hadn't been there earlier.

Picking it up, Lydia read it, and tears rolled down her cheeks.

Zach bunched his brews. "What is it?"

She handed to paper to him. "It's the counter curse for me. I don't have to be a vampire for the rest of my life."

"That's great." He studied her and then added, "Isn't it?"

Lydia nodded. "Yes. But I think I'll wait. At least until the war is over."

Zach scooped her into his arms and carried her to the house. "Whatever you wish. I love you as a vampire or just a healer."

"I love you, too, my dark elf."

He kissed her briefly then teleported them to her room in the Divinity House. He laid her down on the bed and smirked. "Your elf, huh?"

"Yes. You're mine. Just as I am yours."

One side of his sensual mouth lifted. "Always."

EPILOGUE

*I*t'd been a month since Zach and Lydia had closed the portals with Hecate. They still hadn't heard from Lex or Desiree. Not even the *Porter's* mother had heard anything. Ayden and Zach had to go break the news to Eleese regarding what had happened in the Underworld.

Eleese felt that her daughter was still alive. And Jagger said the same thing about Lex. Both of who would know the moment they passed. The magical family bond was strong.

"Does anyone know where to begin to look for them?" Lydia said as she paced in front of the window.

Khloe sat at the desk, using the computer. "Demetrius kept records of the Dark Divine. It'll take time to go through all the files, though. Oh, wait."

Everyone's attention turned to the computer genius. "What?

"A *Porter* child, age ten. Evolved as planned..." Khloe stopped reading out loud and drew her brows together. "Oh, this is crazy."

"For the gods sake, what?" Zach said and walked to her.

Jagger chuckled. "It's your funeral, elf."

Zach flipped the Death Demon the bird and read the file over Khloe's shoulder. "Holy fuck."

"Yep." Khloe read the rest of it for everyone else and then said, "The kid evolved into a changeling. He was able to take any form at will. Plus, he still had the power of a full-blood *Porter*."

"Fuck. Khan will use the kid to create a damn army." Zach straightened and ran a hand through his hair.

Lydia growled. "I bet wherever the kid is, is where we'll find Khan and Samoan."

"And Lex and Desiree," Jagger added.

Khloe held up a hand. "I have a location."

Jagger nodded to Ayden. "I say Khloe, Zach, Lydia, and I go."

Ayden glanced at the four of them and nodded. "Agreed. Kris and I got it here."

"Very well." Jagger glanced to his mate. "Are you going to share the location?"

She shrugged. "I heard the Rocky Mountains are beautiful in the winter."

Zach moved in close to his mate. "We vote to leave on the first flight out." He wrapped an arm around Lydia's waist and kissed her forehead. "Are you okay with that?"

She met his stare. "Yes. I saw Logan this morning. I'm good for a few hours."

His heart ached that she still didn't feel her son was safe enough. Hugging her closer, he whispered, "This will all be over soon. Then we can bring Logan home where he belongs."

And Khan, as well as Samoan, would get what is coming to them.

Get updates on releases via Lia's newsletter
https://www.subscribepage.com/authorliadavis

ABOUT LIA DAVIS

USA Today bestselling author Lia Davis spends most of her time writing racy romance and witty women's fiction, the majority of which takes place in fantasy worlds full of magic and mayhem. She prides herself on her ability to craft strong and sassy heroines, emotionally intelligent alpha heroes, and rich, expansive universes that readers want to visit again and again.

She is the mastermind behind the bestselling Ashwood Falls Series and the co-author of the beloved Witching After Forty Series.

She currently resides in Florida where she's working on her very own happily-ever-after with her supportive husband and spends her free time doting on a pack of feisty felines and her loving family.

Find all of Lia's online hangouts here:
https://solo.to/authorliadavis
Check out the official Davis Raynes Merch Etsy Store:
https://www.etsy.com/shop/davisraynesmerch

ALSO BY LIA DAVIS

Paranormal Women's Fiction

Witching After Forty (Co-written with L.A. Boruff)

Fanged After Forty (Co-written with L.A. Boruff)

Shifting Through Midlife (Co-written with L.A. Boruff
and Lacey Carter)

Packless in Seattle

Paranormal Romance Series

Shifters of Ashwood Falls

Bears of Blackrock

Dragons of Ares

Gods and Dragons

Dark Scales Division (Co-written with Kerry Adrienne)

Shifting Magick Trilogy

The Divinities

Witches of Rose Lake

Coven's End (Co-written with L.A. Boruff)

Academy's Rise (Co-written with L.A. Boruff)

Wolf Ranch